KU-414-661

SMILE

RODDY DOYLE

LARGE
PRINT

First published in Great Britain 2017
by
Jonathan Cape
an imprint of Vintage Publishing

First Isis Edition
published 2018
by arrangement with
Vintage Publishing
Penguin Random House

The moral right of the author has been asserted

Copyright © 2017 by Roddy Doyle
All rights reserved

A catalogue record for this book is available
from the British Library.

ISBN 978–1–78541–510–4 (hb)
ISBN 978–1–78541–516–6 (pb)

FLINTSHIRE SIR Y FFLINT	
C29 0000 1223 207	
ULV	£15.95

C29 0000 1223 207

Just moved into a new apartment, alone for the first time in years, Victor Forde goes every evening to ꞁnnelly's pub for a pint. One evening a man in ꞁ꞊ and a pink shirt brings over his own pint and ꞁs ꞁown. He seems to know Victor's name and to renꞁꞁber him from school. Says his name is Fitꞁꞁtrick. Victor dislikes him on sight; dislikes the mꞁꞁries that Fitzpatrick stirs up of five years beꞁꞁ taught by the Christian Brothers. He prompts othꞁꞁ recollections too — of Rachel, his beautiful wiꞁ ꞁho became a celebrity, and of Victor's small ꞁꞁꞁ to fame as the man who says the unsayable on tꞁ ꞁadio. But it's the memories of school, and of ꞁ particular Brother, that he cannot control, and ꞁꞁh eventually threaten to destroy his sanity . . .

SPECIAL MESSAGE TO READERS

THE ULVERSCROFT FOUNDATION
(registered UK charity number 264873)
was established in 1972 to provide funds for
research, diagnosis and treatment of eye diseases.
Examples of major projects funded by
the Ulverscroft Foundation are:-

- The Children's Eye Unit at Moorfields Eye Hospital, London
- The Ulverscroft Children's Eye Unit at Great Ormond Street Hospital for Sick Children
- Funding research into eye diseases and treatment at the Department of Ophthalmology, University of Leicester
- The Ulverscroft Vision Research Group, Institute of Child Health
- Twin operating theatres at the Western Ophthalmic Hospital, London
- The Chair of Ophthalmology at the Royal Australian College of Ophthalmologists

You can help further the work of the Foundation
by making a donation or leaving a legacy.
Every contribution is gratefully received. If you
would like to help support the Foundation or
require further information, please contact:

THE ULVERSCROFT FOUNDATION
The Green, Bradgate Road, Anstey
Leicester LE7 7FU, England
Tel: (0116) 236 4325

website: www.foundation.ulverscroft.com

For Dan Franklin

CHAPTER
ONE

I stayed up at the bar a few times but I didn't want the barman thinking that I needed someone to talk to. I sat in a corner near a window but the barman kept coming over, casually walking past, looking for empty glasses, and asking me if I was all right for a drink or what I thought of Brazil getting hammered by the Germans or of Garth Brooks not coming to Croke Park. I tried to picture myself from where he'd been looking at me. I can't have looked that bad — that lonely, or sad. Or neglected. It never occurred to me that he might be gay. I was fifty-four. I was too old to be gay back.

There was another place, the Blue Lagoon, a bit further away at the other end of the street. I hadn't gone in but I didn't like the look of it from the outside. It was always too busy. Full of families and couples and groups of men who looked like they talked serious rugby.

I can hear her.

My wife.

— Grow up, Victor.

So I stayed put and decided that Donnelly's was my local. I'd never really had one before. There were three or four pubs within walking distance of the old house

— the house I'd just left — but I'd never homed in on one. I'd been in each of them only a few times over the years and I don't think I'd ever been on my own. Rachel had always been with me.

I went to this new place every night — or, every evening. I had to force myself to do it at first, like going to the gym or to mass. I'd go home — home! — cook something, eat it, then walk down the straight line to the pub. For one slow pint. I'd bring a book or my iPad with me.

Donnelly's.

It was a good old-fashioned name for a pub. I was living near the sea again and I'd gone past the pubs I'd known when I was a kid. The Schooner, the Pebble Beach, the Trawler. They were all a drive away from the apartment, or a long walk that I didn't want. Or too close to where I'd grown up. That would have been sad, a man of my age going back to some wrinkled version of his childhood. Looking for the girls he'd fancied forty years before. Finding them.

Donnelly's would be my local. I trained myself to feel that it was mine. I listened out to hear the names of the staff. My barman, the lad who was on most evenings when I wandered in, was called Carl. Or Carlo, by those men and women who seemed to know him quite well. I kept it at Carl.

— How's himself?

— Not too bad, Carl.

— Same book.

— It's a big one. I'm nearly done.

— Any good?

— It's okay.

— What's it about?

— Stalin.

— There was a fucker.

— God, yeah.

— Worse than Hitler. They say.

— A monster.

— Who'll win tonight?

— Costa Rica.

— D'yeh think?

— I've my fiver on them.

— What're the odds?

— 6 to 1.

— Not bad for a two-horse race.

— That's what I thought.

— We'll be cheering for them, so.

Going into the bookie's was new too. Or just pretending to go in. I hadn't put anything on Costa Rica. I knew nothing about horses or greyhounds but I'd stick the occasional fiver on the football. The winner, sometimes the score. There was a Paddy Power right beside the pub. It became — even just walking past and having a look at the World Cup odds in the window — part of the rhythm of my day. Another corner of my new home.

I'd moved in in the summer, so it was all done in daylight. Waking up, getting out, coming home, climbing the stairs, opening a window, cooking the dinner, strolling down to Donnelly's. A pub in daylight is a different place — it's less of a pub. It's a good time to start, a good time to move in. I could sit back for a while and watch the room become a pub. I'd nod at men I'd seen before.

— The heat.

— Unbelievable.

The apartment — the block, from the outside — reminded me of my old primary school. The car park at the front even looked like a deserted schoolyard. The wood of the main door was a bit rotten where the paint had gone. The door glass had chicken wire running through it. The stairs up to the first floor were wide enough for gangs of charging boys. And there was something about the light that came through the high window at the stairwell in the morning — it seemed exactly like the school stairs more than forty years ago. It wasn't an unpleasant sensation.

My old primary school was only a couple of miles away. The secondary school was even nearer.

The apartment was okay. I'd decided that almost immediately, even when it was empty and bare, and the letting agent — a nice young one, in her early twenties — had let me in to see it. It was going to do.

— Fresh paint, I said.

— Yes, she said.

— Was there blood on the walls?

She looked at me, to make sure I was joking. I wasn't sure I was. But she smiled.

— It just needed, like. Sprucing up.

— Fine.

I wondered if the last tenant had died in here. In the kitchen section of the one big room, or in the bedroom

I'd glanced into. Or the bathroom. But I didn't ask her. I knew it would sound creepy. And I didn't really care.

— I'll take it, I said.

— Oh. Cool.

— Am I your first client?

— Fourth.

— Does your dad run the business?

— No.

— Sorry, I said. — I'm being stupid.

— It's okay.

There were two windows. I looked out one of them and saw the car park, the low railing, trees, and the red-brick houses across the street.

I pointed down.

— Cats, I said.

There were two of them — three of them — sitting under a Renault that looked like it hadn't been moved in a long time.

— They're all over the place, she said.

She stood behind me.

— But they don't do anything, like.

— Grand.

I moved in two days later. I brought a bed from the old house, and the Roberts radio that had been in our bedroom. The clothes I wanted filled one case. My sister brought me a kitchen table and two chairs. I drove out to Swords and got a TV, an armchair and a fridge in Harvey Norman's. I drove down to SuperValu and bought three of their big bags full of stuff — coffee, teabags, soup, apples, bananas, washing-up liquid, a scourer, washing powder, brown bread, a baguette, tomatoes, salt. I half filled my new fridge and put things up on the corner shelves. I put the salt on the table and started my first shopping list.

Pepper etc.

I sat in the armchair and watched Germany versus Ghana, and felt happy enough. I decided my neighbours were prostitutes. Before I saw any of them. There was something about the apartment block; when it wasn't a school — when I wasn't on the stairs — it was East European, Soviet era. I was taking my trousers off the first night when I heard laughter above me, a woman laughing. She was being paid to laugh. It made some kind of sense. I was folding my trousers but I was living dangerously. Behind enemy lines. Somewhere in the building was the whore with the heart of gold, waiting for me. She'd see what my wife couldn't see, and fuck me. For nothing. And cook for me. Or let me cook for her. *Pepper etc.* We'd watch football in bed. I'd hide her from her pimp. I'd get my son to beat him up.

I was there three days, on my way down the stairs to my new local, before I saw a neighbour. He was coming up the stairs, dragging a man-bag, like a big, balding schoolboy. He looked at me and nodded. He was twenty years younger than me, and sweating.

— Great weather, I said.

He didn't answer. I heard his door open — he didn't knock; he wasn't visiting a prostitute — before I pulled open the front door.

The next morning I saw my first woman. I was looking out the window at the seagulls. Someone had left the lid off one of the black wheelies, and a gull had hauled a chicken carcass out of the bin and dropped it. There were three gulls fighting for it, and another gang attacking the bin. The cats were under the Renault, waiting. A taxi pulled up, out on the street. There was the usual delay, a back door opened, a bare foot, then the rest of the woman got out. She leaned against the low railing and put on her shoes as the taxi crawled away, up the street. She straightened up and walked into the car park. She was young — very young. Her knees, in particular, looked very young. She walked like she had no weight. I stood back — I didn't want her to see me looking down. But I could see that she looked happy. I heard the front door — nothing else. She was a prostitute's daughter, I decided. Being given the chances her mother had never had.

It was like the chicken had exploded in the car park. The fight between the gulls had become a major battle for wings and bones. The noise of them — I've always loved it. I looked at the cats. They hadn't moved but they were tenser, braced. A window above me opened.

— Fuck off —!

A man. He'd learnt to say fuck off quite recently. I wondered why he hadn't shouted something in his own language. And I was glad he hadn't. What I'd just seen and heard had been great — the gulls, the cats, the girl, her knees, the shout. It had been wonderful. I had no one to tell it to but I didn't mind that.

I looked at my phone; it was twenty to six.

Milk — small carton.

Bin bags.

★ ★ ★

— Victor?

I looked up when I heard my name but I couldn't see a thing. I was sitting near the open door and the light coming through was a solid sheet between me and whoever had spoken. My eyes were watering a bit — they did that. I often felt that they were melting slowly in my head.

— Am I right?

It was a man. My own age, judging by the shape, the black block he was making in front of me now, and the slight rattle of middle age in his voice.

I put the cover over the screen of my iPad. I'd been looking at my wife's Facebook page.

I could see him now. There were two men on the path outside, smoking, and they'd stood together in the way of the sun.

I didn't know him.

— Yes, I said.

— I thought so, he said. — Jesus. For fuck sake.

I didn't know what to do.

— It must be — fuckin' — forty years, he said. — Thirty-seven or -eight, anyway. You haven't changed enough, Victor. It's not fair, so it isn't. Mind if I join you? I don't want to interrupt anything.

He sat on a stool in front of me.

— Just say and I'll fuck off.

Our knees almost touched. He was wearing shorts, the ones with the pockets on the sides for shotgun shells and dead rabbits.

— Victor Foreman, he said.

8

— Forde.

— That's right, he said. — Forde.

I had no idea who he was. Thirty-eight years, he'd said; we'd have known each other in secondary school. But I couldn't see a younger version of this man. I didn't like him. I knew that, immediately.

— What was the name of the Brother that used to fancy you? he said.

He patted the table.

— What was his fuckin' name?

His shirt was pink and I could tell that it had cost a few quid. But there was something about it, or the way it sat on him; it hadn't always been his.

— Murphy, he said. — Am I right?

— There were two Murphys, I said.

— Were there?

— History and French.

— Were they not the same cunt?

I shook my head.

— No.

— Jesus, he said. — I hate that. The memory. It's like dropping bits of yourself as you go along, isn't it?

I didn't answer. I have a good memory — or I thought I did. I still didn't know who he was.

He moved, and put one foot on top of a knee. I could see right up one leg of his shorts.

— Anyway, he said. — It was the one who taught French that wanted your arse. Am I right?

I wanted to hit him. I wanted to kill him. I could feel the glass ashtray that wasn't there any more, that hadn't been on the table since the introduction of the smoking ban a decade before — I could feel its weight in my hand and arm as I lifted it, and myself, and brought it flat down on his head.

I looked to see if anyone had been listening to him. I could hear the remains of the word "arse" roll across the room. I hated this man, whoever he was.

But I nodded.

— Fuckin' gas, he said. — And look at us now. Would he fancy us now, Victor?

— Probably not.

— Not me, anyway, he said.

He slapped his stomach.

—You're not looking too bad, he said.

His accent was right; he came from nearby. He took a slurp from his pint — it was Heineken or Carlsberg — and put the glass back on the table.

— You've done alright, Victor, he said. — Haven't you?

I couldn't answer.

— For yourself, like, he said. — I see your name all over the place.

— Not recently.

— Fuck recently.

I wanted to go.

—You did great, he said. —We're fuckin' proud of you.

I wanted to move house, get back across the river. Home.

—Victor Forde, he said. — One of us.

A minute before he'd thought my name was Foreman.

— You married that bird, he said.

I shouldn't have, but I nodded again.

— Fuckin' hell, he said. — Good man. There's no end to your fuckin' achievements.

— Who are you? I asked.

He stared and smiled at the same time.

— Are you serious?

— I know your face, I said.

— My face?

He laughed. Straight at me.

— My fuckin' face? he said. — Jesus. I was — what? — seventeen. The last time you saw me. Am I right?

I didn't know — I didn't know him. But I nodded.

— Will I give you a hint?

I didn't nod this time.

— Síle Fitzpatrick, he said.

The name meant nothing.

— Who?

— Go on — fuck off.

— I don't know her.

— Síle. Fitz. Patrick.

— No.

— You fuckin' do, he said. — Wake up, Victor. Síle. You fancied her. Big time. All of you did. She was a bike. Síle Fitzpatrick. She was *the* bike. Yis all said it.

I hadn't heard that phrase, "a bike", in years. It was like a piece of history being taken out and shown to me. A slightly uncomfortable piece of history.

— No, I said.

— Blonde bird, tall, Holy Faith, Bowie fan, woman's tits.

She was starting to come together; I thought I was remembering someone.

— You all fancied her, he said again.

— And you didn't?

— Well, I did. But I couldn't.

— How come?

— She was my sister, he said.

The laugh exploded out of him, as if he'd been holding on to it for years. There was nothing funny in it. The girl was in my head now, Síle Fitzpatrick, but I wished she wasn't. I wanted to tell him that I didn't know her. But I could see her sitting on the low ledge outside the chipper, her back to the glass. I was inside, looking at her hair, her shoulders, her white uniform shirt tucked into her skirt. I wanted her to turn and look in. I wanted her to look at me.

— You remember me now, I bet.

I didn't. But I remembered his sister.

— Yeah, I said. — I do now. Sorry.

What was his name? He'd been in my class for five years; he must have been. Fitzpatrick, Fitzpatrick.

I had it.

— Edward.

— Good man, he said.

I knew him, and I'd known him years ago. I knew his face and I'd known his face.

— Eddie, I said.

— I kind of prefer Ed these days, he said. — More adult.

He shrugged.

— Finally had to grow up, he said.

What he'd told me just before he'd laughed — one of the words came back and nudged me.

— You said "was". You said she *was* your sister.

— Yeah, he said.

— Was, I said.

— Yeah.

— Sorry — I said. — I don't — She's not —?

— Dead?

— Is she?

— No, he said. — No. We're not close, just.

— Oh.

— Yeah.

— Grand.

— Say no more, says you.

The gap was beginning to close. "Say no more, squire" — the Monty Python line was straight from the schooldays.

— You meeting someone? he asked me now.

— No, I said. — No. Just having a pint.

— Same as myself. D'you live near here, so?

I hesitated. I didn't want to explain.

— Or just visiting? he said. — Slumming it for a bit.

— No.

— No?

— I live down the road there — five minutes.

— Oh grand, he said. — So this is your local.

— Not really.

— Fuck this, he said.

He stood up and picked up his stool; he'd scooped it from under himself before he was upright. I didn't have time to cower. But he turned to the table beside us and lowered the stool one-handed while he grabbed a chair with the other and dragged it across to him. He sat down, and back.

— That's better.

There was even more of his leg on show now. He didn't seem to be wearing underwear.

— So, he said. — Yeah.

I waited.

— I was away myself for a bit, he said.

— Were you?

— Yeah, he said. — Here and there. Nothing special. But Sile. She'd love to hear from you.

He'd guessed it: Sile was the only thing I liked about him.

— I hardly knew her, I said.

— Go on to fuck.

— It's true.

— Yeah, yeah, he said. — She fancied you. Big time. Had me plagued. *Is he going to college? What's his favourite Bowie song? Is he going with anyone?* A right pain in the arse.

— "Heroes", I said.

— What?

— My favourite Bowie song.

He laughed. He sat back, almost lay back, and barked at the ceiling. There was grey pubic hair poking out of his shorts. He sat up, adjusted his crotch. Had he caught me looking at him?

— D'you know what? he said. — I'd say she'd still be interested in knowing that.

— What?

— Síle, he said. — She'd love to know that "Heroes" was your favourite Bowie song. I don't believe that, by the way. Now maybe, but we're talking about — when? 1975 or '6. "Heroes" was released in 1977. So you're spoofing. As usual. You can fuck off, so you can. Vict'ry.

I should have stood up.

— Remember we used to call you that? he said.

I should have just left. He might have followed me but I should have walked out and kept walking. I'd have been giving nothing away. Because I found out later, he already knew where I lived.

CHAPTER
TWO

I was so bored, so heavy with the physical weight of it, I could have cried; I could have stopped breathing. At the same time, I was often terrified and I laughed so much I went blind. I went to the school, St Martin's CBS, for five years and I had an erection for four of them, even during Irish. I sat through *Peig* and *Ò Pheann an Phiarsaigh* and thought of legs and nipples and the birds on *Benny Hill* and my friends' mothers and sisters. And the women in the *Sunday World*. And the pictures of footballers' wives that were sometimes in *Football Weekly*. And Lynsey de Paul. And the women in Abba. And Pan's People. I rode the desk, or I tried to.

Moonshine was sitting in the desk behind me. He jabbed at my back with his Doc Marten.

— Right, Vict'ry, he whispered. — Go on. Your time has come.

— Fuck off, I whispered back.

— Go on.

— Fuck off.

— Quiet at the back, said Brother Murphy.

He was up at the front, writing the homework on the blackboard. He wasn't as savage as most of the other

Brothers and lay teachers. Just now and again, he lost the head. Something would snap and there'd be no warning. He'd headbutted Cyril Toner when there'd been almost total silence in the room. I'd been doing French comprehension, thinking of French girls' mouths sucking the words, when I heard a kind of thump, and a groan. I looked up. Murphy was staggering back, holding his forehead, and Toner just stood there. His hands were hiding his nose. He was squealing and there was blood coming through his fingers. Dripping. It was frightening and cool; it was history. *Christian Brother Loafs Student.* And — this was the vital part — he hadn't loafed me. Relief, shame, joy. Toner was a wanker.

And nothing happened; there were no consequences. Toner went home with a broken nose after Murphy sent him to the Head Brother's office. And Toner would have felt lucky when he got out of the Head Brother's office without being assaulted again. That was the thing: it wasn't assault. Not back then. It wasn't what most of us saw at home and it wasn't what we'd experienced in the national school, the primary school. But I never thought I was witnessing anything illegal. Even being felt up by a Brother was just bad luck or bad timing. Toner wouldn't have told his parents. He'd have given them a story. A football in the face, or a hurley, a slammed door, an elbow; the school was full of good, believable ways to break your nose. They'd have all laughed about it in the Toner kitchen. The Head Brother hadn't brought him home or to the

Mater A&E. He'd just been sent on his way. The Brothers knew they were safe.

But fuck Toner. It wasn't my nose. Fuck him. Murphy wasn't the worst. Although he liked me.

That was why I'd been kicked in the back by Moonshine.

— Make him smile.

— Fuck off.

Brother Murphy was about forty-five, but it was hard to put an age on adults. I never saw them as younger or older than my father. All men seemed to be that age. But it wasn't the age; it was distance. They seemed far away, in another room or country. Men — not just the Brothers — had nothing in common with us. I didn't understand them. And I wasn't alone. My mates were with me: all men were fuckin' eejits.

Brother Murphy was small, the same height as most of us. But he was wide. He came through the door sideways. His hair was cartoon black. It might have been dyed, but that wouldn't have occurred to us. He had a head and a jaw like Desperate Dan's. But he enjoyed his subject and he loved talking to himself in French at the top of the room. We, the pupils, never spoke French. We read and wrote but learning to speak wasn't on the curriculum. There was one day, he was at the front of the room reading from the Inter Cert book. I can't remember its name but there was a skinny boy called Marcel — the book had illustrations — and he lived in a place called Saint-Cloud. I remember watching Murphy and thinking, "He wishes he was there." He wanted to be a Frenchman. He wanted a beret and a Renault, and a son called Marcel. He was happy in the book. I'm older than he was back then and I think I recognise it now: he was miserable. He was lonely.

And this violent man with the Desperate Dan head liked me. I knew this — everybody knew this — because of something he'd said more than two years before, when I was thirteen.

— Victor Forde, I can never resist your smile.

It was like a line from a film, in a very wrong place. I knew I was doomed.

It had been one of Murphy's happy days and we were at him to let us off homework for the weekend. It was Friday afternoon and the sun was heating the room, spreading the smell. The school was right beside the sea and we could hear the tide behind the yard wall.

— Go on, Brother.

— *S'il vous plaît*, Brother.

— We'll pray for you on Sunday, Brother.

He listened to us and grinned. It was a grin, not a smile. The word "inappropriate" didn't appear until years later. But the grin was inappropriate. It was all inappropriate. He was being taunted and teased by a room of boys and he was loving it.

Then he said it.

— Victor Forde, I can never resist your smile.

There was silence.

It was late September. I'd only been in the secondary school for three or four weeks. I hadn't even got the hang of it. All the different teachers, the size of the older boys, the violence and the constant threat of it.

19

And the place itself was a maze; the school was actually a row of large red-brick houses. The trip from Geography to Science involved leaving one room, going through another room after knocking at the door and enduring the sneers and kicks of the fifth-years; out to the yard, into another house, through what must originally have been the kitchen door, down a hall, and left, into a science lab that had a bay window with a view of the railway embankment and a huge fireplace. And thirty Bunsen burners. And a mad chain-smoking prick in a white coat leaning against his desk. Every day was exhausting. Exciting and upsetting.

The silent response to Murphy's declaration would eventually have to end. But I hoped it wouldn't. There was still the possibility that he hadn't said it. While the silence lasted. But it ended.

Someone exhaled.

Everyone exhaled. Murphy had turned his back on us. He picked up his personal duster and rubbed out the homework.

— You win today, boys, he said. — No homework.

— He fuckin' fancies him, Derek Muldowney, sitting beside me, whispered.

Him, not *you*. Muldowney shifted away from me. I wanted to pull him back. *It's nothing to do with me!*

— He's a queer.

— You're a queer.

— Murphy knows you're a queer.

— I wasn't smiling, I told them. — I wasn't.

He'd been looking at me — Murphy had; he must have been — all that time. *I can never resist your smile,* he'd said. *Never*. He'd seen me when I'd walked in the front gate on the first day. The Brothers' house was beside the school. All the Brothers lived in there. Murphy must have been looking out the window of his bedroom, at all the new first-years as they arrived. And he'd decided that I was the one. There were boys in the class who still looked a bit like girls. Or there was Willo Gaffney, who said he had to shave twice a week. There was Kenny Peters who had a scar on his forehead and was absent from school every time the Circuit Court came to the GAA club. I couldn't see why he'd picked on me. I wasn't like a girl or a man. I'd no big brothers; no one had warned me about him. *Never smile back at him. Never get ten out of ten. Never get below five — don't give him any excuse to keep you back after the bell.*

I'd gone into a school that was a row of big, detached houses, with black gates, a neat hedge and trees that looked as if they'd been planted hundreds of years ago. I'd walked out of our estate — there'd been five or six of us, together — where most of the trees hadn't survived, where some of the footpaths hadn't been finished. I hadn't been in there half an hour before I'd been hit, lifted by an ear and dropped, been called an eejit by the prick in the science lab because I thought he was pointing at someone else; I'd got lost and ended up in the senior yard and got kicked by a gang of lads who wouldn't have touched me, or even noticed me, outside school. But I wasn't alone. We were all thrown, all the first-years, all around the place. We suffered together and it was great. Then, last class, first day,

21

before going home to my mother's questions, the French teacher, Brother Murphy, smiled at me, the first adult to smile all day, and I smiled back.

— And you are?

— Victor Forde.

— Victor Forde, Brother.

— Sorry, Brother.

— Have I had the pleasure of teaching any older Fordes? Any Defeats or Armistices?

— No, Brother.

I was pleased; I'd remembered to call him Brother.

He smiled again.

— Fine, he said.

He put a finger on my shoulder — it was just a strange little friendly, comical nudge — and pointed to a desk halfway down, under the window.

— You'll sit there.

— Thank you, Brother.

He smiled. But he'd smiled at all of us.

— Have I had the pleasure of teaching any older Kellys? he asked Moonshine.

— Yes, Brother.

— Oh, God help us.

He didn't mind when we laughed.

— So, said my mother when I got home.

She was excited, young; she'd never gone to secondary school, herself.

— How was school?

— Great, I said.

I meant it.

Her eyes were wet.

— I'm so proud of you, Victor.

She picked up my sister to make her kiss me, then made egg and chips to celebrate the occasion. I couldn't wait to go back in the next morning.

But then Murphy singled me out. He'd been smiling at all of us but then he'd announced that I was the one whose smile he couldn't resist. I knew the others were going to kill me. I knew it as I began to understand what Murphy was saying and what it meant. I knew the lads would destroy me after the bell went and we were outside. And they did. They didn't even have to wait until we were outside the school grounds. The Brothers never minded violence. There was no point in trying to avoid it. I was surrounded, pushed.

— Yeh fuckin' queer.

— I didn't smile.

A schoolbag — a Leeds United kitbag — was swung high and into my back. It hurt but I laughed. The slaps became thumps. They were all over me now. But it wouldn't last; I knew that too. I was kicked, punched, spat on. For a minute. Only a few of the kicks really hurt, and the thumps were just to my arms and chest. No one thumped or kicked me in my face. The spitting — we did that all the time.

It was over. There was space around me. They'd drifted away. Only my real friends stayed behind. They laughed. And I laughed. I could breathe. It was over. Moonshine handed me my schoolbag. Doc picked my jumper up off the ground and walloped the muck off it.

I was sick when I got home. I put my mouth right over the bowl, so the vomit wouldn't splash too much.

I waited in the bathroom until my eyes looked normal again. I put on my jumper, so my mother wouldn't see the bruises on my arms.

And it wasn't over at all. I was stuck with it, what Murphy had said; I became the Queer.

— Murphy's in his moods.

— We'll get the Queer to smile at him.

— Go on.

— Fuck off.

I was the Queer for forty minutes a day three times a week, and for an hour and twenty minutes on Fridays, right through the first year. My mother never noticed how I started to feel sick on Thursday evenings, about once a month — I knew what I could get away with. She never spotted the pattern. I was sick on Fridays but I ran to school on Tuesdays. We didn't have French on Tuesdays.

But staying away didn't work. I was miserable because I wanted to be in school. I wanted to be with the lads. And it didn't work because, nearly three years later, I was still the Queer and Murphy still couldn't resist my smile.

— Smile at him.

— Fuck off.

— Go on.

I didn't know — and I still don't — why I changed my mind that day, why I decided to give up and accept the role. I don't think it was a real decision. I just felt it — surrender.

I put my hand up and clicked my fingers.

— Brother?

I heard Kenny Peters.

— For fuck sake.

I was suddenly, unexpectedly, delighted. I was frightening even Kenny Peters. I did the click business again.

— Brother.

— *Oui?* said Murphy.

He turned from the blackboard to see who wanted him. At the same time, I heard the Canadian geese flying over the school, and honking. It was early April.

— The geese are going home to Canada, Brother, I told him. — Spring is in the air.

I wasn't looking at anyone else but I knew they couldn't believe what they were hearing. I was actually being the Queer, talking about spring and the geese.

— So, I said. — Any chance you'll let us off the homework tonight, Brother? To celebrate the departure of *les canards*.

— That's ducks, yeh fuckin' eejit, Moonshine whispered.

No one laughed. They knew I'd gone too far. They waited for Murphy to charge down to my desk, forehead first.

I smiled at the Brother; I grinned.

He looked at me, then away. He stared at nothing — at the wall beside the broken statue of the Blessed Virgin. She had a hole in her back but the Brothers didn't know that. She'd fallen from her perch when Willo Gaffney had dragged the teachers' desk over to her during a free class. He'd climbed up and taken his langer out, to make her give him a blowjob. She fell off,

25

sideways. We caught her, all of us, but Muldowney's knee had gone through her back.

Murphy stared at the wall, then spoke.

— Take down the homework.

No one pleaded with him. No one spoke. The bell went.

He left.

We got off for Easter a week later and, the first French class after the holidays, a woman walked into the room.

— Jesus.

— A woman.

— *Une femme.*

— Say no more, squire.

— *Une femme jolie.*

— Bleedin' hell.

It was unbelievable. Literally unbelievable. A woman had walked in from the world outside. The real world. We saw women all the time; our lives were full of women and girls. But this was the first time a woman had come into the school. The cleaners didn't count. We never saw the cleaners. Moonshine's mother was a cleaner but he was always home before she went up to the school.

The woman walked in. She put a bag on the desk.

— She's a teacher!

— Where's Murphy?

— Dead.

— Is Brother Murphy dead, Miss?

— *Non.*

She was French or she was pretending to be French.

26

— Is he sick?

— *Non*.

— Is he gone?

— *Oui*.

Jesus.

— Why, Miss?

— Silence, please.

They shut up for a bit and stared at her. I knew what had happened before they did. I'd got rid of Murphy. I was going to claim it. *I expelled the fuckin' zombie.* I didn't know exactly how it had happened, but I knew it had. I'd smiled back at him and he'd panicked; I'd pushed him out of the school. He was never coming back.

It wasn't the end of the school year; there were seven weeks to go. The Brothers were always moved during the summer holidays. The ones who were too violent or the ones who put their hands on boys' necks and left them there. The ones who stood at the classroom window and said nothing for forty minutes. They'd be gone, or some of them would, and there'd be a few different old zombies and one or two younger, mad-looking fuckers walking around the walls of the yard when we went back in September. But this was different. It couldn't wait till the summer.

I could see Murphy's suitcase. I could see him in the back of the Brothers' minivan, after dark, lying on the floor so he wouldn't be seen as it skidded out onto the road and they smuggled him to safety.

Something had definitely happened.

They were all staring at the woman. She was at the board and she was holding a bit of chalk. I could tell, she didn't want to turn her back. But she'd have to, if she was going to write her name on the board. That was what they always did, the new teachers.

She was going to have to do it.

It was first thing in the morning. This must have been the first class she'd walked into. The Head Brother hadn't come in to introduce her. He always did that with the new teachers and the temporary ones. He'd come in and warn us. He'd once grabbed Doc and battered him at the front of the room, because he'd said that Doc was smirking. He'd been telling us who the new teacher was and he'd grabbed a hold of Doc before he'd finished and pulled him out from his desk. The Head Brother's hands were huge and he'd hit Doc four times on the head with one of them, and shoved him, kind of thrown him, back onto his desk.

— That's how we deal with go-boys in this school, *a Bhráthair*, he'd told the new Brother, and us. — Some of these gentlemen think they're in Butlin's.

But he didn't come in with the new teacher this time. He didn't want to face us. He didn't want to answer questions, even though no one would have asked any. He didn't want to see the faces or the glee. The woman was looking at more than thirty boys — I forget the exact number — looking back at her. She'd probably had it all planned in her head, how she'd write her name, then get us all to introduce ourselves in French. She might have taught in a different school, in France. But this was the first time she'd been stuck in a room like this one. The room was savage, even when it was empty.

She wanted to run. She wanted to get up on the ledge and climb in behind the Blessed Virgin. She'd climb into the hole in the Virgin's back.

I heard something. A zip. The low groan a zip made when it was being opened slowly. Sometimes silence was louder than noise. The silence thumped the sides of my head. It hammered me and the whole room.

I looked to the side. I didn't see properly but I saw enough — the looks on other faces, shock, joy, absolute fuckin' terror — to know. Just behind me, across the narrow aisle, Kenny Peters had his cock out, under the desk.

I'm not like that, I wanted to tell her. *I'm not like that at all*.

I'd smile at her. I'd welcome her to Ireland. I'd carry her bag to the bus stop. I shuffled forward a bit and rode the desk.

CHAPTER
THREE

— What are you up to these days? he asked.

It was the question I dreaded, and I could have dodged it. I could have stayed at home or gone elsewhere. But I hadn't. I'd come down to the same pub, Donnelly's, at the same time in the evening. I'd brought a book with me. I'd left the iPad in the apartment because I knew he'd eventually pick it up and start fucking around with it. The point was, I knew we'd be meeting again and I'd done nothing to avoid it.

He picked up the book, and lobbed it back on the table.

— Scoping the opposition? he said.

He'd come in soon after me — like the first time we'd met. If I'd stayed up at the bar it would have been different. There'd have been the punters coming and going, and Carl the barman. Fitzpatrick would have been distracted. He was constantly shifting and looking around; he'd have got involved in other conversations. But I'd let this happen. I was sitting at the table near the door, where he'd found me the first time.

I put my hand on the book and pulled it a bit closer to me.

— No, I said. — Not really.

— Fuck off now, he said. — It must be dog eat dog, the writing game. With the Amazon and the Kindles and that. Books are fucked, I heard.

He hadn't looked at the book cover. Anyone else would have asked if it was any good.

— Go on, he said. — What are you up to? You creative types — fuckin' writers. You must always be working on some fuckin' book — I'd say, are yis?

He was wearing the shorts I'd seen him in the first time and I thought the shirt might have been the same too. I'd searched for Síle Fitzpatrick on Facebook and I'd found lots of her, dozens of Síle Fitzpatricks. The first one had been a teenager in Tralee. I'd stopped looking.

—The urge must be there all the time, he said. — Is it? To be writing something or other.

He knew I'd fall for it.

— Not really, I said.

That was true but I loved thinking — even lying — that it wasn't.

— Is that right? he said. —Well, I know if it was me. If I was able to write a book — if I had it in me. I'd be churning them out. It's a fuckin' gift really, isn't it? Do you know how many books I read a year?

— How many?

— None.

— None? I said. — At all?

— Fuckin' none, he said. — I'm not proud of it.

But he was.

— I tell people I'm dyslexic, he said. — But I'm just a shiftless cunt, really.

He shifted in his chair just as he said "shiftless". He sat forward, then pulled himself back. He held on to one of the chair legs.

— And the gas thing is, it works. People relax a bit when they think I'm dyslexic. Not that anyone gives much of a shite. But they don't have to pretend they know a lot. It lets them off the hook or something. And me.

He coughed.

— And I'll tell yeh, he said when he'd finished. — More than a few leg-overs have come my way cos of my fuckin' dyslexia.

He burst out laughing. He really did. His face expanded, for a second.

— So you haven't read my book, I said.

— No, I fuckin' haven't, he said.

His head went back; he laughed again. Everything about him was abrupt, a bit violent. But the laughter was different this time; he'd decided to laugh.

I hadn't a written a book, although I'd met people who claimed they'd read it. Some of them had even liked it. I knew he wasn't going to be one of them.

— What do you do, yourself? I asked him.

I knew nothing about him, other than the facts that he'd been in my class in school and he had a sister who I'd fancied but couldn't really remember.

— I'll tell you, Victor, he said. — I'm between things.

He sat up noisily and leaned forward, almost as if he was going to sip the head off my pint.

— I got out of one thing, he said. — No blood on the floor. And I'm kind of going into another.

He made it seem like he'd told me something, that he'd given me insider information.

— What was the thing? I asked him.

— The writer, he said. — Always digging. For fuck sake, will yeh look at your one.

His eyes, and half his body, followed a woman who'd just walked in, across the path of light at the door. Her friends, all women, were behind her and they went right past his face as he turned. A scarf — one of those light ones that I'd noticed women wearing all summer — slid across the top of his head.

— More of them, he said. — Happy days, Victor.

He didn't care if they heard. He wanted them to hear. I thought at first that he was trying to avoid my question, but he wasn't.

— Where were we? he said.

He kept staring at the women. He turned in his chair, as if he was thinking about getting up on his knees. The women were all in their early forties, I guessed, old school or college friends on their way home from work or out for the night. The latter, I decided. They weren't dressed for work. They were all trying hard to look like they hadn't tried hard. It was my wife's look.

— The oul' MILFs, he said. — You can't fuckin' beat them. The bit of madness, the bit of experience.

He was still staring at them.

— I was in the building game, Victor, he said, and turned to watch the words hit me.

He smiled.

— Do you feel soiled? he asked.

The fucker knew me.

— No, I said. — Not at all.

— We were to blame for fuckin' everything, he said.
— Weren't we? The builders and the bankers. We
brought the whole country to its knees.

He slapped one of his own knees.

— But, he said. — I'd say, going back, you were pals
— you and your missis, like — I'd say you were buddies
with one or two builders. Back in the day. Am I right?

— One or two, I said.

That was true. More than one or two. Although we'd
thought of them as developers. Adventurers. Warriors.
Chancers. We'd known some of the men who'd brought
their kids to school in helicopters. The only thing about
Fitzpatrick that made him one of those men was his
shirt.

— Good man, he said. — You know the road outside
— if you turn left and go on down to the sea?

I nodded.

— You know the big hole in the ground, on the right?
Where the row of red-bricks used to be?

— I know where you mean, I said.

It was a gap in the houses, hidden behind a wooden
hoarding that had buckled and sagged.

— That was my last hurrah, he said. — Think of me
the next time you're going past that fuckin' hole.

— Okay.

— Good man. I don't own it any more, of course. I
don't even own this hole.

He leaned to the side and slapped his backside. The
pub stopped till the noise faded.

34

He grinned.

— Sure, fuck it.

He looked over at the women again.

— It was good while it lasted.

He looked at me.

— I was a millionaire, Victor, he said. — Can you credit that? I never got round to buying the yacht but I had the fuckin' brochure. I was a phone call away.

The laugh burst out again. The face blew out, and quickly fell back into place.

— For fuck sake, he said.

He coughed, and laughed again.

— Anyway.

He looked across at the women again.

— The blood is up, he said. — D'yeh fancy a slice yourself, Victor?

My throat was dry. I wasn't going to give him an answer. I didn't trust my voice. *Yes*. *No*. I wanted to run.

I stayed where I was.

He looked at me, and back at the women, and at me.

— The one on the left, he said. — She'll do me.

He settled back into the chair.

— You're a lucky man, Victor, he said.

— Why?

I knew what was coming.

He used a thumb to point at the women behind him at the bar.

— You've one of your own at home, he said.

I said nothing.

— Haven't you?

I looked across at the women. I hoped it might distract him, make him jealous, that he'd go all alpha and block my view or even get up and bring his pint across to the bar. But, if I'm being honest — and I'm still not sure that I am — I welcomed his provocation. It felt close to slagging. I hadn't been properly slagged since I'd left school. I didn't like Fitzpatrick and I still couldn't remember him; I couldn't picture him in the classroom, sitting beside me or standing at the top of the room, getting slaughtered by a Brother. But there was something about him — an expression, a rhythm — that I recognised and welcomed. It was why I was sitting there.

— A fine-looking bird, he said. — I never miss her when she's on. That one she's in. *Operation Transformation*, is it?

— *Hit the Ground Running*.

— That's the one. What age would she be now?

— Fifty-two, I said.

— A bit younger than you.

— Not much.

— No, no. Fair enough. You're — what? — the same as meself.

— Fifty-four.

— The magic fuckin' number. We're getting old, Victor. We're already fuckin' old. She'd be made up and that, dolled up for the cameras. Wouldn't she? They all are, I suppose. They have to be. Am I right?

— Yes.

— Still though. A fine-looking bird.

I thought for a while that he wanted me to thank him.

— She must've been unbelievable back in the day, he said.

— We're not together any more, I said.

There it was. Out.

— Ah, no, he said.

I nodded.

— Ah, I'm sorry, Victor, he said. — I'm sorry now to hear that.

I felt good and devastated. And excited. It went way past thinking that I was getting it off my chest. I was announcing something new. It didn't matter that I was talking to a man I didn't know or like. It made me strangely giddy. The people who knew were people who hadn't needed to be told. People who'd lived with us or near us. This was the first time I'd told someone outside the circle, since I'd stepped outside the circle.

It was done.

— Are you back home with your mother? he asked.

I shook my head. I enjoyed shaking it.

— No, I said. — No. Actually, she's dead.

His face got ready before I'd finished speaking.

— Ah, God — shite. More bad news.

— Four years ago.

— I never knew, he said. — Sorry.

— Thanks, I said. — Yours?

— Dead these donkey's years, he said. — Both of them. My da, God rest him, died when I was still in school. D'you remember?

I tried to — I tried to remember the day, the news, him being called out of the class, like I had been. I tried to remember his father's funeral. But all I could recall was my own experience, walking out of the school, home; the curtains drawn, my mother crying and smiling, my uncle putting his hand on my shoulder and leaving it there; sitting alone on my bed, freezing; standing at the side of the grave, feeling the ground, the soil, loose beneath me, scared I'd slide or topple in on top of the coffin. My own father had died when I was still in school. I didn't remind him.

— Fifth year, he said.

— Yes, I said.

I remembered nothing about it. I suspected that there was a lot I couldn't remember from that time when my father wasn't well. He'd died when I was in fifth year, same as Fitzpatrick's — in February. Perhaps it explained why I couldn't remember Fitzpatrick.

He looked across at the women. They were still there and — to me — unusual. It was a long time since I'd seen women in a group like that, in a loud, sexy clump.

— Is your da gone as well? he asked.

He was still looking at the women.

— Yes.

— Before your ma?

— Yes, I said.

— Seems natural that way, he said.

He looked at me.

— The man before the woman. Do you know what I mean?

— Yes, I said.

38

He smacked his stomach — reminded the pub and the women that he was there.

— We might get the sympathy vote, beyond, he said.
— A pair of big orphans.

He took his glass and stood up. I couldn't follow him. I wanted to — but I wasn't sure about that. I wanted to go over, to get in there among the women. I wanted to lean against them, make them laugh. But I finished my pint, grabbed my book and got out.

CHAPTER
FOUR

My wife was well known. *Is* well known. Ever since I've known her — and it's been more than thirty years — whenever there's been a newspaper feature on successful Irishwomen, my wife's name has been one of the first to be trotted out. The look, the style of the piece is familiar, and so is the list. There is the politician, often a junior minister; an athlete of some sort, Katie Taylor or one of the women's rugby team; there's a CEO, a nun or an ex-nun, a woman who has done something big, saved children or animals; there is a restaurant or club owner, and a judge; the recent additions are a black woman or an Asian, a successful gay woman, a woman with a disability, and a gorgeous woman with seven or eight kids. There is always the group photograph. My wife has been in the photographs for more than thirty years and she'll be in there until she no longer wants to be. It will be her choice.

When we met, we were neck and neck. We met outside a studio. I was on my way to becoming a successful man. I never became one. But she quickly became the woman who was famous for being successful and she has remained that woman.

Her name is Rachel Carey.

Yes.

I never really came near to be being successful, although in Ireland you can get along for a long time before the truth starts to matter. *You're never off the telly.* That was often said to me years after the last time I'd been on television, and years after I'd stopped being a regular on Sunday-morning radio. Two appearances in close proximity make you a regular in Ireland — or, in Dublin. So my three or four panel performances got me there. I was famous for a book I was writing but didn't write. I got away with that for three or four years. Then I was famous, but less famous, and far less interesting, for being a bit of a mouth. Rachel, though — Rachel was famous for her achievements. And, for a while — a short while — we were famous for being us.

When we met I was a writer. I'd written some things for a magazine — now gone — called *What Now*. It sold about eight thousand copies every month and was basically a music mag, with extras. I wrote record and gig reviews, although I actually wrote about myself. We were encouraged to do that.

— It's not a gig, the editor, Charles Jacob, told us. — It's you at a gig.

So I wrote about a day out in Slane, and Bob Dylan just happened to be there too. He was supporting me. I pretended I was Hunter S. Thompson, but only when I was writing, three days after I got home. In my mother's kitchen. I'm being hard on myself. I was a kid and, years later, people still told me how much they'd enjoyed that piece, even though they often mixed me up with other writers and that gig with other gigs. But that was what I did. My review of the Smiths at the SFX was an account of me surviving a night in the north inner-city. My review of R.E.M. at the SFX was another dangerous stroll through Nighttown. I gave myself six hundred words; Michael Stipe got two hundred, fifty more than Morrissey.

What Now was supposed to be what the *NME* had been in the mid and late 70s, but it had nothing like the bigness. Lou Reed never had an argument with anyone from *What Now;* we never got near Springsteen or, really, anyone who's still listened to today, or even heard of. "We" were four or five young men and a woman who were in and out of the two-room headquarters on Hanover Quay. We were paid very little. I remember getting a cheque for five quid for my review of *October*, and going into the Bank of Ireland on College Green to cash it. My name was on the review, but it was "we" who wrote it. We sat in a bedsit and scrutinised it, shouted our opinions over the songs, until they became one opinion. I don't think I ever heard that record properly. But I still called it a classic, or something like that. I had to. We never said it, but we wanted to become indispensable to U2. We wanted to be their friends, and we hated them for that. And we were too late. U2 were gone before we started. So we wrote about the new U2s, as many as we could find, or could find us. We adopted them — championed them, tried to keep up with them, wanted to be them, until it became clear that they weren't going to follow U2, and we'd move on. To another band, and another couple of months of A&R gossip and freezing rehearsal rooms and schoolgirls doing their homework while they waited for their boyfriends to stop torturing their instruments and notice them.

Torturing their instruments — the language of an old man. That wasn't what they did; it wasn't what I heard. They were brilliant and I envied them all, because I couldn't do it. I could write a bit. I'd seen a woman laugh at something I'd written; she'd looked up and smiled at me. I could put a word beside another word and make them surprising; I could imitate the men who wrote in London and New York. But I could never stand on a stage or even in a corner of a rehearsal room or garage. I tried it a few times. I sidled into a space and hoped the band wouldn't notice that they'd gone from four to five, or hoped they would and wouldn't object. They'd give my backing vocals the thumbs up, or nod and grin as I shook new sounds from a tambourine. But I'd always crawled away before the hope had time to form. No one told me to. I just couldn't do it. Expose myself. Open my mouth, let noise come out. I was shy.

There was a time when writing was more important than the music. That was long before I started, but I was happy pretending to be Dublin's Lester Bangs — much happier than Lester ever was. I didn't really do the drugs and a little man inside me slapped the walls of my stomach whenever I tried to go past four pints. I was happy and miserable, a fraud who objected to being one, and I was quietly honest with myself. I didn't want to be the one who wrote about the music and that was what gave the words their energy and zip. I drank while I pulled the pint away from my mouth. I hated and loved, and envied and sneered.

A singer stood in front of me once, and cried. His name was Gerry Finglas. It was his real name. He found me in a pub near the Ha'penny Bridge. I was there spending the eight quid I'd been paid for reviewing his last gig.

— Why? he asked.

I looked up at his face and knew he wasn't going to hit me. He was a softy off the stage. I'd grown up with lads who hit you. I knew the body language, and the eyes. I was safe here.

— Why what? I said.

I wasn't alone; two other guys had cashed their cheques with me.

— Why did you write that?

I'd seen him swinging a mic stand in a packed basement, people on the stairs, right up, out to the street. He didn't see the heads in front of him, or care. I remember a girl's screech above the other screeches.

— Fuck me!

She meant it and she wasn't even looking at him. She couldn't. And here he was in front of me, crying. *Jim Morrison meets Joe Dolan*. He could never get that out of his head, and it killed him. He accepted it. I'd turned him into a joke he told himself every time he stood at the side of a stage waiting to go on. Because I envied him. No one else had paid much attention to what I'd written. They laughed at it — *Jim Morrison meets Joe Dolan* — but thought it was quite affectionate, an Irish

44

thing, and forgot about it. More and more people were coming to watch him sweat. But the sweat was Joe Dolan's now and he tried to stop it. He started to wipe his neck with a white towel. I'd called him "a better, taller Bono". I wrote that his band, the Liffey Snakes, had "crawled out of Them's grave". I said he didn't sing about sex; he *was* sex. He was Jim Morrison. *Meets Joe Dolan*. He was perfect and I made him ridiculous. He died ten years ago.

I meet them sometimes, ex-members of ex-bands. I meet them accidentally; I've kept in touch with no one. It started at the school gates, waiting for my son to come out. I'd be standing beside someone I'd known years before. We'd smile before we remembered who exactly we were. And we'd keep smiling as we caught up with ourselves.

— For fuck sake — is it you?
— You still playing?
— No.

It's funny — those words, "years before". There were nine or ten years between the brat with a borrowed typewriter who lived at home with his mother and the stay-at-home (sometimes) father, and between Dublin's hottest bass player and the self-employed tech consultant (or something), both waiting for their children to come out of their Educate Together school.

— How many have you?
— Just the one — yourself?
— Three.
— Jesus.
— I know.

Those nine or ten years yawned — a gulf, a different time and world. But the twenty years since feel like a couple of months.

I feel so far away.

I can't seem to believe, or cling to, much of what I know I'm remembering, even though I know it happened. I was bored — I remember that. I was sick of being the observer. There was never any sex. I was too shy and too stupid. I never knew if I was attractive. I didn't object when I saw myself in a mirror, in my mother's house — I hadn't started to think of it as my mother's house; I still lived there — or in the rare pub toilet that had both a working light and a mirror. But I began to hate hearing myself, and I stopped talking. I was tired of being angry too, sick of it. Because it was never the real thing. I'd gone to UCD, University College Dublin. It was miles away from where I lived. Across the city, across the river, across a border of expectation. I was the first in my family, both sides, to have any kind of third-level education; we didn't know what the phrase, third-level education, meant. I was years out of college before it occurred to me that that was what I'd had. And I never felt proud of that, and not because I didn't graduate. I was just angry — and vain. Angry. Always angry.

Later on, I blamed the Christian Brothers. But back then, I'd forgotten all about them.

I didn't finish the degree — History and English. I didn't drop out. I just went less, and less. I'd been published. I didn't have to write my final-year dissertation or sit the exams. I was already a writer.

I wrote two record reviews and sent them in to *What Now*. Both were accepted. I discovered that when I bought the latest edition, Bob Marley on the cover, and opened it. There was the first one, my three hundred words on *Remain in Light*, in the top left-hand corner of the first of four pages of album reviews. "Talking Heads have reinvented themselves. And reinvented music." That was something I'd heard someone say, in someone else's kitchen. We were listening — half listening — to a bad tape of the album. The second review was right below the *Remain in Light* one, thirteen words on a twelve-inch single by a Dublin band called Dresden Playground. I remember it by heart, because I read it so often. "See review of *Remain in Light*, above, and place 'not' before every verb." I knew Dresden Playground. Their drummer was in my history tutorial, in first year. I'd gone to their second gig, upstairs in the Merrion Inn. They were good; they were grand. But they were there because this was their neck of the city and their parents had bought them their instruments and gear, and there was talk of a van for the UK tour. But that wasn't why I hated them, because of all the spoons I put into their mouths. I didn't hate them. I envied them, and that was far worse. They could do it, and I couldn't. It was the start of my career, and I tore into them with thirteen words. It was the making of me.

I went into *What Now* the day after I'd seen my first words in print. I wasn't sure if I was going to be paid. But I was — six quid. I watched the girl behind the desk go into a room and come back out with a docket for me to sign, and a small pile of records for me to review. There were "Not for Sale" stickers on them and I immediately felt chosen. I showed them to my mother. I showed her the reviews. She read my name at the bottom of each and that was enough for her. I showed her the cheque for six punts. She laughed. She kissed the cheque, like she'd seen it done on television.

— Your dad would be so proud of you, she said.

Was that true? I didn't know. He had died only five years before, but I didn't know him. My mother had reacted exactly as I'd known she would but I had no idea how my father would have looked at me or what he would have said. I saw his photograph every day but I could never hear his voice or see him move across the kitchen.

I'd had three more reviews in *What Now* when I decided that it was what I needed to do, much more than I needed to finish a ten-thousand-word dissertation which I'd been calling *What if He Hadn't Been Shot? James Connolly's Death and the Irish Revolution*. I'd made a girl laugh and touch my arm when I'd told her that I was thinking of rewriting it as a musical after the finals. But I couldn't look at her while I spoke. I could look at her, briefly, and say nothing. Or I could make her laugh while I looked over her shoulder or at a wall. I couldn't do both. But I could write. I'd seen my name in print, so I could call myself a writer. I'd seen others do it and they wrote fuck all. A published poem could get you ten years. I wasn't greedy; I just wanted a couple of months. I got that, and a bit more. It was exciting. For a while. It's the phrase that seems to capture everything about me, then and now — "for a while".

"For a while", now, means the twenty-first century. But when I try to remember myself at twenty or twenty-one, and the excitement that came with being thought of as a writer, "for a while" was a year and a couple of months. "For a while" was the months before the final exams I didn't do, and the summer, up to Christmas and the new year, across the anniversary of my first published review, and the slow acceptance that it wasn't enough. As I became more savage — the word seems daft, but it's accurate — it gave me less. There was an honest bit of me that wouldn't let me get away with it, even as I was getting away with it — just about. I was doing nothing.

It wasn't how I'd been reared. My parents had worked hard. After he died, I was told again and again — I *knew* — my father had always worked hard. Everyone I'd grown up watching had worked hard. The people I knew and loved worked hard and talked about it, and ate to do it and slept to be ready for it. I don't recall ever thinking that this was bad, or a waste, or an injustice. I remember my mother stretching, straightening her back after she'd been bent over, putting sheets and pillowcases through the mangle that was attached to the washing machine, and smiling at me. She'd groan too sometimes, picking up my sister or pulling the pram up the steps into the house or, later and more frequently, just doing things around the house. She kissed my father and listened as he ate his dinner and told her about the kind of day he'd had and she told him something about her own. They worked hard and loved each other. That rhythm still seemed to be there after he died. I grew up with hard work.

It got to me, finally. I was suddenly terrified, and miserable. I've no idea how I would have ended up. I've often seen myself on a park bench, trying to sleep. It's a waking dream; I'm not sure if I've dreamt it while asleep. I'm trying to sleep, I'm freezing and wet, dawn is crawling over me. I'm curled up but my legs hang over the side of the bench. I'm rigid. Caught. I think I'm in London. Ridiculous, I know. Self-pity, I know. And sentimentality. I think if I'd let it roll a bit further, I'd have sat up and taken a notebook from my jacket pocket. I'd have started writing notes, even fully formed sentences. I'd have turned into George Orwell, if I'd let myself. Because it's bullshit. It scared me the first time but I grew to enjoy it. I even told a woman about it once, and she cried — and burped.

I was savaging kids who were getting younger than me by the month. I'd become a bully. The something — the resolve — that had let me send in those first pieces, put them in the envelope and post them; that resolve — it was something like that — or ambition; whatever it was, it was gone. Ambition was a decision, not a trait. There were no more decisions. I couldn't think of anything that I could do. I'd run out of friends and their bedsits. I noticed — and I still can't quite accept that it took me so long to see it, although I've never been quick — that when I thought of "we", it had become "I". "We" were still there but "they" had actually moved on. They were writing about football

50

now too, and politics. Or they moved to London, even New York. They were actually writing. I'd no interest in politics and I'd moved far away from football. They intimidated me, and I dismissed them. I told myself I didn't care; I forced myself to believe that. But I think of it now, and I realise it hurt.

I got drunk alone one night. No one came near me. I smiled — I think I smiled; I remember I did, or tried to — at a woman. I remember the tightness around my mouth. I remember trying to cop myself on. I remember trying to decide to stand and bring my pint across to her.

I saw her years later.

I was with my wife in the car. It's not that long ago.

— I went with her once, I told Rachel.

— Who?

— Her — at the pedestrian lights, look. She's pressing the button.

She was almost thumping the button. But I didn't know why she was demanding permission to cross the street; the traffic wasn't budging and she could have strolled through the cars. I didn't point this out to Rachel; she didn't like me demeaning people, especially women.

— Which one? she asked.

I saw now that the woman was with a teenage girl. They both looked angry. The girl was looking away from her mother — it was definitely her mother. There was another woman — she was about forty. This other woman was behind my fictional old flame and her daughter, trying to work her way past without touching them. That was who Rachel meant; she wasn't sure which of the women I'd meant. The woman, *my* woman, looked a bit unhinged, as if she was in a world she didn't know. She was thin *and* overweight. She wore Uggs like her daughter's.

— With the teenage kid, I said. — Reddish hair — see?

I was driving but we'd been stuck on Westland Row, outside the Dart station, for ages.

— With the coat?

— Yes.

— She's lovely, said Rachel.

She said that about virtually all women her own age. She meant it, always, but she knew it wasn't true. She wanted it to be true.

— What's her name?

— Vickie, I said.

It wasn't the first time I'd pointed out a fictitious old girlfriend. Women who'd aged well, some who hadn't. Rachel loved it. I've no idea where the name, Vickie, came from but I remember I'd had it ready, somehow, for when I'd need it.

The traffic ahead of me jumped a few feet and I followed it. I knew I was safe. Rachel wouldn't roll down her window and call to Vickie and her daughter. *Recognise him?* Warmly and a bit triumphantly. She loved me and believed me — and believed in me — for years.

— When was that? Rachel asked, as the traffic moved again and kept moving.

— Just before I met you, I told her.

— The girl isn't yours then, she said.

She smiled — I could see her while I looked ahead and got us onto Merrion Square. She was grinning at me — for me. We laughed.

CHAPTER
FIVE

He didn't knock. He just opened the door and stepped in. He didn't shut the door or say hello to Brother Connolly, Patch, our maths teacher.

— Stand up, he said.

We knew who he was; we'd heard all about him. Tom Jones. He got that name because chest hair crawled out the top of his shirt and someone had once heard him singing in the teachers' toilet.

We all stood up. Beside the desks. The way we were supposed to.

Tom Jones stood in front of Toner.

— Doh — reh — mee — fah —

Tom Jones was singing. We couldn't laugh, and that made it even better. He charged up the scale.

— Soh — lah — tee — *dohh*!

Then he pointed at Toner.

— Sing.

Toner got to mee, then stopped. I couldn't see his face but it looked like he was crying.

— Sit down, said Tom Jones.

Frankie Best was next.

—You.

Only three lads in the class had broken voices and Frankie wasn't one of them. He'd played Prince Charming in the Christmas show in primary school.

He sang.

Tom Jones nearly smiled.

— Outside, he said. — And wait there.

Patch was sitting in his chair, under the Virgin. Frankie passed him on his way to the door.

— That was lovely, said Patch.

— Thanks, Brother, said Frankie.

Tom Jones stood in front of every boy in the room and made them sing the scales. Ten of us were sent out of the class. I was one of the last.

— Out.

When you left our class, you walked straight into the yard. It was raining. There was a little porch but only a few could fit into it. I tried to get a corner but I was shoved off the step.

— What's he going to do to us?

— Don't know.

— I'm not joining a bleedin' choir.

But we wouldn't have a choice.

Tom Jones came out.

— This way.

We followed him into the other house, the senior side of the school. We had to go through a sixth-year class but no one kicked us this time. We went after Tom Jones, up a stairs we'd never been on before, and then another, a really narrow one, and we walked into a room with a sloping ceiling. We were right in under the roof of the school. It was amazing, a mix of light and dark. There were no desks, no blackboard, just two chairs. And about forty lads from all the other years. We were still a bit scared but we felt it — I knew it: we'd been brought into a club, where we could stand beside and talk to the older lads, where we were almost their equals.

Tom Jones made us sing the national anthem that first day. He got us to stand in three lines and he walked between the rows. He'd grab the shoulder of a jumper and pull the boy into a different line, in front of or behind him. He hit a sixth-year when he didn't move fast enough. He thumped the side of his jaw and pushed him back, to the back line. They called the sixth-year Mungo because he had sideburns down to his mouth, like the singer from Mungo Jerry. He was bigger than Tom Jones but he did nothing. It was the most frightening thing I'd seen. And we had to keep singing the national anthem.

Tom Jones stood beside me.

— Louder.

I tried. But I kept forgetting the words. I'd learnt them years before, when I'd been about six. The words were Irish; I'd never really known them properly and I'd never known what all of them meant. Tom Jones's chin was down at my shoulder. I could feel his breath on the side of my face. He grabbed my jumper and pulled me across, to the edge of the front row.

He stood in front of us now. He held his right hand high, then he sliced the air as he brought it down, across his chest. We could hear his grunt, and we all stopped singing.

— That was dreadful, he said.

Some lads at the back laughed. It seemed to be okay.

— Tomorrow, said Tom Jones. — Nine o'clock. Here.

He pointed at Moonshine.

— When?

— Nine o'clock, sir.

He pointed at another boy.

— Where?

— Here, sir.

— Remember exactly where you are standing, said Tom Jones. — I will not be reminding you.

He pointed at me.

— You.

I had no throat. It had gone. I'd never be able to speak.

Then he moved his finger to Frankie.

— You.

He pointed at about eight of us, five in the front row and three behind us.

— You are sopranos, he said. — Get out.

We had maths with Patch the next morning at nine but we went up to the room under the roof. We'd hardly spoken about what had happened, or what was going to happen. I wasn't sure if being in the choir was a good or a bad thing. I wondered if being sopranos would get us murdered by the older lads. We were ten minutes early. We didn't do anything. We didn't even put our schoolbags in a corner. We just waited.

— Were you in the choir before? Frankie asked a third-year.

— What choir?

— Is this the first one?

— Looks like it.

We heard the bell. We heard doors close, and the end of the shouting below. We were above the normal life of the school. We said nothing.

No one was late.

Tom Jones came in and shut the door.

— *Dia dhaoibh.*

— *Dia is Mhuire dhuit, a mhúinteor.*

— I don't need to bother with a roll call, he said.

He pointed at Moonshine.

It wasn't me, it wasn't me.

— Have you heard of Seán Ó'Riada?

— No, sir.

— You are a fool. What are you?

— I think I might have heard of him —

— You are a fool!

Tom Jones hadn't moved. I could feel Moonshine's terror, the heat of it. I could feel him shivering beside me. I was shivering too.

Seán Ó'Riada had composed a mass, or music for a mass, in Irish. And we were going to learn it. First or last class every day, we'd go up to the room under the roof and learn to sing Ó'Riada's mass.

The next day, after the second rehearsal, we found out that Patch was gone. Someone's big brother had seen him fainting the day before, on the path between the school and the Brothers' house. Patch was ancient. You could see his bones right under his skin. When the sun was bright and he was standing near the window, it was hard to make out his face.

We hadn't seen the new teacher yet, but we knew: he was in the school, somewhere. This was nothing like a free class. The door was open, but no one was going to close it. The Head Brother would be coming in with the new teacher. No one was going to be caught out of his seat.

The Head Brother was impressive. He could walk into the room, scan us, and know exactly what was going on. If we'd done our homework, or how things were at home. He never shouted; he never had to.

He walked in now. He stared.

The new guy was with him, right behind him.

— Gentlemen, said the Head Brother.

He looked at everyone.

— Brother Connolly will not be with us. For the foreseeable future. Do you know what that means?

He pointed.

— Do you know what that means?

—Yes, Brother.

— And if I told you to tell us what it means — now. Would you be able to?

—Yes, Brother.

—Would you?

—Yes, Brother.

— I'm inclined to believe you, said the Head Brother. He had us slaughtered, on the slab; we were terrified and grateful.

— This is Mister McDevitt, he said. — And he will be your maths teacher — for.

He pointed.

— The foreseeable future, Brother.

— Exactly, he said. — The foreseeable future. I'll leave you to it, Mister McDevitt. They're a good bunch of lads beneath it all.

He walked the few steps to the door.

—Victor Forde, he said, without stopping. — Follow me.

I'd done nothing. My homework, all of it, was in my bag. I was in the new choir, my clothes were clean, I'd got my hair cut the week before.

He was waiting outside. He'd stepped out of the porch, and turned. I stood now on the step. We were almost the same height; I wasn't looking up at him.

— Shut the door a minute, he said quietly.

I did, and faced him again.

— How is your father? he asked.

— Fine, Brother, I said.

— Good, he said. — Good man. He's in our prayers, tell him. And your mother. Back you go, inside.

— Thanks, Brother.

We called the new guy Super Cool, because he thought he was cool and he wasn't.

— Must try harder, said Doc.

He didn't bother whispering. Super Cool had just tossed his bit of chalk onto the tray under the blackboard, and missed. The chalk hit the floor and Super Cool tried to look like he'd meant it. He shrugged and sat on the teachers' table. None of the teachers ever sat on the table. When he got up a bit later there was chalk on his arse. We could see inside his briefcase. Sandwiches in tinfoil and a flask; no books, no newspaper.

60

— Thinks he's Paul McCartney but he wraps his sambos in tinfoil.

It was true, we decided. Super Cool was trying to look like Paul McCartney.

— Here, sir! Will we take that down or let it be?

— Who said that?

— The jailer man and Sailor Sam, sir.

It was the first time we'd given a teacher his nickname. One of Moonshine's brothers heard the name from Moonshine, and Super Cool became Super Cool all over the school. When it was quiet in our room, we'd hear lads somewhere else singing "Band on the Run" or the end of "Hey Jude", and we'd know who was trying to teach them.

Tom Jones never got any less frightening. I never got used to him. He never smiled but there were days when you knew it was all right to laugh when he said something or when one of the older lads couldn't get to the right note. He wouldn't come at us with his fists. But sometimes we got it wrong. It would be okay to laugh one minute, then someone would be bent over, holding his arm where Tom Jones had thumped him. I'd watch tears drop on the wooden floor and I'd love Tom Jones because they weren't my tears.

One day, a second-year's voice broke halfway through one of the hymns, *Ag Críost an Síol*. He stopped being a soprano and became an alien. He kept singing; he probably hoped the one-note frog voice would go away, that his boy voice would come back. Before Tom Jones got to him.

Tom Jones lifted his arm, and sliced the air. We stopped singing, bang on.

— Was that you, O'Driscoll?

— Yes, sir, sorry, sir, Derek O'Driscoll croaked; he whispered, terrified of the sound.

Moonshine nudged me. There was going to be killing.

But there wasn't.

— Congratulations, said Tom Jones.

He let O'Driscoll stay in the choir, even though he couldn't sing.

We didn't know why we were learning to sing Ó'Riada's mass. Tom Jones never told us and we couldn't ask him. No date was mentioned, no Sunday in the future when we'd be singing it in the parish church. We didn't care. The free classes were great, and being in a kind of club. Tom Jones only hit me once. He walloped me across the head with the rolled-up sheet music. It didn't hurt but I thought I was in for more; he stood right behind me for ages — for ever. I couldn't sing. I couldn't move. But I was still glad I was there because I was missing French.

One Friday, he told us we were to come in the next day, all day, Saturday, for practice. No one said anything. No one groaned or put up his hand. There'd be no football, or anything else. I went to the library on Saturday mornings. I'd bring my father's books back and pick three new ones for him. I wouldn't be doing it this week.

We were all there on Saturday morning. We had to wait outside the school gate until one of the Brothers saw all of us and came out of the Brothers' house and unlocked the gate. Then we had to wait again at the main door until Tom Jones arrived in his car. He was wearing O'Connor's jeans and a cravat.

— Bleedin' eejit, Moonshine whispered.

We were in the room under the roof for about half an hour when there was a knock on the door. We looked at Tom Jones's face and hands; we were to keep singing. The door opened. I could see Brothers outside. They looked like they were wrestling. There were three of them, and one of them was Patch. He was being helped by the other two, Brother Fay and the art teacher, Brother McConkey. McConkey — Conkers — had his dog, Setanta, with him. Setanta was always covered in paint, where lads had cleaned their brushes on him.

Patch was even frailer than the last time he'd taught us. I thought the Brothers were carrying him. He was wearing his soutane, and I couldn't see his feet; they might have been inches off the floor.

Tom Jones lifted and dropped his arm. We stopped singing and watched.

The Brothers sat Patch down on one of the chairs. I could see his feet now. He was wearing slippers. I could see pyjama bottoms too.

His smile was terrible.

— Hello, boys.

— Hello, Brother.

— *Dia dhaoibh.*

— *Dia is Muire dhuit, a Bhráthair.*

Then Tom Jones made us go back to the beginning and we sang all we'd learnt. Tom Jones didn't stop us.

He just stood at the front and conducted. He didn't look angry and he didn't sweat. It struck me then; he was on his best behaviour.

Setanta barked once but we didn't laugh. Conkers kicked him and put him outside the door. Conkers was as old as Patch and he sometimes honked. You could tell; he didn't know he did it.

We kept singing and got to the end.

— Thank you, boys, said Patch. — That was lovely.

It took him ages to say the words, like each one of them had to be pulled out of his mouth. His eyes were wet. They looked even worse because the skin around them was red and flakey. He tried to stand up. The other Brothers pulled and carried him to the door. Tom Jones didn't move. One of the Brothers got the door open and Patch turned, as much as he could, so we saw the side of his face.

— I'm looking forward to it, boys, he said.

He fell over Setanta but the two Brothers caught him and we thought we heard laughter after the door was shut again, and a yelp.

We knew now: we were rehearsing for Patch's funeral. We couldn't wait to get out, so we could talk.

— Bloody hell.

— He nearly died when we were singing, did you see?

— Can't blame him, your fuckin' voice.

I told my mother about it. She sat down.

— That's so sad, she said.

I was surprised. I'd expected her to be a bit more concerned, even disgusted. They were making us sing for a zombie. There were old horror films on BBC2 every Monday night and I was allowed to stay up and watch them, by myself. Most of them were boring but I loved talking about them the morning after, with the other lads who'd seen them or pretended they had. I'd remember every bit, to catch out the lads who were spoofing. I'd describe scenes that weren't in the films, and trap them. I was being a prick, but it gave me power and I had no other way of getting it. In the middle of the werewolves and vampires and the various Frankensteins, there was one film, *Night of the Living Dead*. It was different. It scared me. It wasn't made of cardboard and the ones getting out of the graves, the zombies — the living dead — seemed real. They *were* real. They were ordinary people. They weren't exactly ordinary but they were only slightly warped. What they reminded me of — the men among them, dragging themselves, never giving up — was the Brothers. That only became funny when I said it the following morning, but it never really stopped being worrying and possible.

— But he's not dead yet, I told my mother.

She nodded, but she was looking out the kitchen window.

— Are we going to see Dad today? I asked.

She shook her head.

— Tomorrow, she said.

I was relieved and that made me feel terrible, and still relieved.

Patch died the week after that, and we were ready; we knew the whole mass. I woke up with *Ag Críost an Síol* in my head, always in the same place, halfway through, every morning. For years.

We had the day off school, just the lads in the choir. We were to make our own way to the church. It wasn't the parish church, the new church, John the Baptist. Tom Jones told us how to get to the Brothers' own church, where to get off the bus, what corner to turn after we walked down from Fairview.

— Nobody will be late, he said.

— No, sir.

— You will all wear white shirts.

I didn't have a white shirt. My mother got me one the day before the funeral, when I was at school. It was nearly see-through.

— You can wear a vest under it, she said.

I'd stopped wearing vests. I was becoming good at spotting what was cool and what would get you killed.

A gang of us went to the funeral together. Upstairs on the bus; it was great. We didn't care about Patch. Not when we were together and the sun was making us squint, even though it was freezing in the bus. We got off a few stops early. I wasn't sure where we were. We were following Doc because he knew a lane. We liked lanes but there were no good ones where we lived.

— Was Patch dead? I said.

— What d'you mean was he dead? said Moonshine.

— When he came in to hear us, I said. — He might've been dead already.

Moonshine shrugged. There were seven of us walking together. No one thought it was mad.

— What about the others? I asked.

— The other Brothers?

— Yeah, I said. — They might be dead as well.
They're zombies.

I knew what I'd just done. I'd invented something
that would live for years. My own monster, and I was
giving it to my friends, the only people I cared about
and the only people who really, really frightened me,
because of how things shifted, how the wrong word, the
wrong shirt, the wrong band, an irresistible smile, could
destroy you. You had to have something useful, your
size or a temper, or a sister. The Brothers were zombies.
Because I'd said they were.

— The fuckin' Brothers are fuckin' zombies.

— What about the other teachers?

— No.

We all agreed. The lay teachers weren't zombies.

— They're only cunts.

We came out of the lane, onto the Malahide Road. I
knew where we were again. We crossed, pushing and
running, to Griffith Avenue. The Brothers owned all
this. My father had said that the night before, when I'd
gone with my mother to see him in the hospital. He
said he was impressed that mendicants like the
Brothers could hold such vast tracts of land. He'd
made my mother laugh. Then he'd closed his eyes. I
knew: he wasn't asleep. I knew: he wanted us to go.

We walked under huge trees, and past a row of
colossal grey buildings. We found the church. We were
early. But Tom Jones was there, smoking in his car. He
was wearing a black suit and he'd cut himself shaving.
We waited for him to get out, so we could follow him

into the church before the coffin and the Brothers arrived. We stood a good bit away from his car.

I looked at Tom Jones as I spoke, and I made sure the others could see that.

— Can a Brother be a zombie *and* a cunt? I asked.

— Shut up, he'll hear you.

— No, he won't.

I wasn't sure about that. I could see smoke coming out the driver's window. I was squeezing years of risk into a few seconds. I'd never get this chance again. I knew that if I became the centre of the day, I might never have to do it again. They'd still call me a queer but they wouldn't mean it. They might even stop calling me Queer.

— I'll ask Fay in Religion tomorrow, I said. — Excuse me, Brother, are you a cunt or a zombie?

The lads hid behind a few cars and broke their shites laughing. I was thirteen but I felt seventeen, nineteen, twenty-three.

The hearse was coming. We could see it on Griffith Avenue, waiting to turn on to the hill up to the church. Tom Jones got out of his car. He dropped his butt on the ground and stood on it. The lads made themselves visible again. He stared at us, then walked into the church by the side door. He knew he didn't have to tell us to follow him.

The church wasn't full. It was just a load of Brothers and some of the other teachers, and the Brothers' housekeeper, Missis Delaney. And one other woman.

I saw Conkers's shoulders first. He looked like he was laughing but I knew quickly that he was crying.

— They were probably boyfriends, Doc whispered.

It was the worst, and the best. Trying not to laugh. Waiting for the next Ó'Riada hymn, wishing for it, so I could concentrate on the notes and the Irish and Tom Jones's hands, and forget what Doc had said. The smothered laughter was heat. We could all feel it. The church was freezing — it had been freezing for years — but my face was sweating, and right under my arms.

Brother Fay wiped his eyes with his fist. He took off his glasses, and put them back on. Another Brother I didn't know got out of his seat, genuflected, and walked out. We were up in the loft, at the back of the church. I leaned out and saw him taking a packet of Sweet Afton out of his coat pocket.

They didn't carry the coffin. They walked behind two men in black coats who pushed the coffin on a black trolley. Brother Murphy, the French teacher, was down there, near the back of the line. He was looking at the black-and-white tiles as he walked. The woman didn't go; she stayed sitting. The church was empty now, except for the woman and a man at the front who was doing something with leaflets. And us.

— Sir?

It was a sixth-year. Hughie Breslin. He was going with Moonshine's sister. Moonshine said that he had all the Moody Blues' records.

—Yes? said Tom Jones.

— Do we have to go to the graveyard? Hughie asked.

Tom Jones looked up from his sheet music and stared at Hughie.

No one even breathed.

Could a teacher hit someone in a church? Hughie was taller than Tom Jones.

Tom Jones shifted his eyes and looked at all of us.

— No, he said. — You do not.

CHAPTER
SIX

Charles Jacob looked out at me. He was on the phone but he lifted his free hand and called me in. I stood in front of his desk — there wasn't a chair — and listened.

— Ah, fuck off now, Frank. Fuck off. Just — I'm telling you. Fuck right off.

I pointed at the door. Did he want me to wait outside? His eyebrows told me to stay where I was.

— Frank, Frank. I'm putting the phone down. Now. I don't believe a word of it — threaten away there. We'll see — fuck off, fuck off, bye, good luck, fuck off.

He put the phone down, held it a half-inch over its rest, as if still listening to Frank's fading complaints, then dropped it.

He looked at me.

— How are you?

— Grand.

— Good man.

Charles — he was never Charlie — was a good deal older than anyone else in the building. He'd started a pirate station on the North Sea, or he'd been on the boat for a while. *Happy days, happy days. Did you ever try masturbating during a Force 10 gale?* He had a family, kids and a wife, somewhere near — he cycled to work — but I never saw them. He was like a big brother, I think. A much older brother, who I hadn't really known until he came home one day and was suddenly there. Family but strange. Warm, but hard to understand.

— The time has come, he said.

— For what?

— Do you interest yourself in politics? he asked.

— No.

— At all?

— Not really, I said. — No.

I don't know why I didn't just say Yes, and let myself catch up with the lie. Everyone else had done that. The political commentators, the travel writers, the food and wine experts — they'd all happily accepted that they knew much more than they actually did know.

— Well, Victor, he said. — Now you do. You're John fuckin' Pilger.

I liked that. It was immediate, effortless. I knew he wouldn't be sending me to Cambodia. Although I already began to see myself there, walking through the killing fields. I was, I remember, very happy. Charles Jacob had done what years of education had never done. He'd paid me a compliment; it still makes me tingle. I wanted to go home and tell my mother.

I was right. I wasn't going to Cambodia. I was going to interview a politician called Aileen Clohessy. Charles Jacob's wife knew her. They'd met at a wedding. Aileen Clohessy had started crying in the ladies, and she'd ended up talking to Charles. I don't know why he didn't take the job, do the interview, himself. He was all body; he couldn't help it. There was too much of him. Even sitting down, he towered over everyone else, his arms and hands were always in use and up near any ceiling. He was a thug, and aware of it. He took a gamble. He saw something in me — or saw nothing particular in me — and sent me off to do the job. He gave me a phone number, a desk with a phone for ten minutes, and a loan of a tape recorder.

— I'll want it on Monday.

This time I knew exactly what to say.

— Okay.

— Monday morning.

— Fine.

I got her immediately when I called; she was in her constituency office. She spoke as if she knew the call was being listened to, and as if we'd met before. I loved it. I thought I could hear breathing, the operator listening in, or — the thought sat down and didn't worry me — the Special Branch. Charles hadn't told me why I was interviewing a backbench TD but I guessed it wasn't because she liked Echo and the Bunnymen.

— She has something she wants to say, he'd told me.

— What?

— I think you'll probably know it when you hear it.

— Okay.

— Let me know if you don't.

I went to the National Library to do the research and couldn't quite believe it when they let me in. As I left the front hall, and went deeper in, and up, no one called me back. I felt like I was emigrating. I even looked back. There wasn't much to find out. Aileen Clohessy had come back from London and taken her dead father's seat. She'd been in Leinster House just less than half a year.

I put the microphone on its stand, in front of my mother.

— What's your name? I asked my mother.

— Ah, Victor.

— Go on, Mam.

She was delighted. Her son had a job. A real job she could bring to the shops. *Victor's a journalist.*

— Molly, she said.

— Molly what?

— Molly Forde.

— And what do you do, Molly?

— I'm your mother, Victor.

Bringing home that Sony cassette recorder was one of the nicest things I ever did for my mother. I had a job that she understood and that wouldn't have come my way without the education that neither she nor my father had had. The cassette recorder and especially the microphone and its plastic stand were what she'd been hoping for, fighting for, since I'd been born. Charles Jacob was right. In the kitchen of my parents' house, I was John Pilger. In my mother's eyes. I told her I'd be interviewing a politician.

— Oh, Victor.

She gave one of her noiseless little claps. I can see it now; she was great fun.

— Who?

I told her.

— A woman, she said.

— Yeah.

— Be nice, she said.

— Of course.

— Do, she said.

— I will.

—Your dad would be proud.

—Yeah, I said. — Would he?

— God, yes. He'd be floating.

So I met Aileen Clohessy. She was in the hotel foyer, with a pot of tea and the *Independent*. She was wearing a blue trouser suit and her black hair seemed stuck on, somehow, not her own. She looked the part, a Fine Gael TD.

— Is here okay? I asked.

— It's fine, she said.

There were people coming and going but we were in a corner, almost behind a heavy, tied-up curtain. I took the recorder from the case my mother had given me when I'd been accepted for UCD. I plugged in the mic and put it beside her teacup.

— Testing, testing. Just tell me your name, please.

— Aileen Clohessy.

— I'll just check that — sorry about this.

— Take your time.

She smiled when she heard her voice being played back.

— That'll do us, I said. — So.

So.

I did a good job. I have to make that claim, although few who remember the whole thing would dispute it. I need to assert it, to myself — for myself. I felt good throughout. It was like finding a football in the grass and discovering that I could control it, use it precisely and unpredictably. She told me about her father's death — because I asked her to. It was beautiful, asking and then listening as the answer flowed. And it did flow. She spoke of the shock, the phone call from her younger brother to her neighbour's flat in Crouch End; the plane home, gathering the money for the fare from friends and cousins; being collected at the airport, still expecting to be met by her father; the drive west, the devastation, the hurt, still expecting to hear his voice almost a year later.

— What were you doing in London?

— Living, she said.

She smiled.

She worked for London Underground. Advertising.

— The ads on the walls?

— No, she said. — Advertising for the service itself. I started on the Jubilee Line.

She'd loved it, loved London, loved her father. She couldn't remember too clearly the meeting in the good room at home when the big party men had told her that she'd be inheriting her father's seat, that she'd be running in the by-election. She remembered wanting to give her mother a boost; it was the day after the funeral. She remembered wanting to please her father. She remembered realising that the seat would be hers only until her brother had graduated and taken a teaching job in the constituency. Was that alright? the men wanted to know; did she understand? Not really, she told me. She didn't feel there'd been a choice. She'd done what was expected of her, to make some people happy and to make others just go away.

She smiled again.

— How has it been? I asked her.

She made a noise I became familiar with years later. We all do, as we get older around others who are also getting older. The noise was laughter, but mirthless. I thought, and think, she was in pain.

She wasn't a politician, she said. Or, more accurately, she wasn't an Irish politician. She was no good at the clinics and funerals. The night-time driving. She'd got used to city life, the bus and Tube commute — the employee concession and all. She missed London.

She hesitated.

— Boyfriend? I asked.

It was the only stupid thing I asked, I think.

— No, she said. — Just the life there.

She wasn't cut out for the politician's life, she said. It wasn't in the blood, after all. I'd read, I told her, that the other sitting Fine Gael TD in her constituency was very impressed with her. That, she told me, was because she kept her mouth shut, did what she was told, and would never stray into his end of the constituency. She'd known almost immediately that she had no interest in making a name for herself or in being the one the journalists would want to befriend.

— I knew the first day, she said. — When I was brought into the chamber and they stood and applauded. It was lovely. Mammy was in the gallery. And my brother. They couldn't have been nicer. But I just wanted to run away. I was nearly sick — vomited, I mean. I'd never even gone back to empty my flat.

— In London?

— Yes.

It was a nightmare, she said. Literally. She blamed no one.

— What about the politics of it? I asked.

— What do you mean?

— Well, I said. — Do you believe in what Fine Gael stands for?

There were silent seconds then, and I knew she was getting herself ready to cross a line. I remember listening to the tape later, and knowing the hiss was a prelude to something big; and not just later, but then, in the hotel foyer, as the silence was being recorded. There was the sound of a till being opened in the bar, and laughter, two men laughing; I hadn't heard or noticed them at the time. I was looking at her and I knew I'd found my career.

— Some of it, she said.

— Not all of it?

She shook her head.

— What about the referendum? I asked.

It was 1983, just three weeks — I think — before the first abortion referendum.

She seemed to relax. She didn't exactly slump but she looked as if she'd finished saying what she was actually only starting to say.

— It's dreadful, she said. — I hate it.

— Why?

— I had an abortion, she said. — I've never regretted it.

— Does your family know?

She shook her head.

— No.

— And this is on the record?

She nodded.

—Yes, she said. — I'll tell them.

She'd had the abortion six years before, when she was a second-year student in UCD. She'd had a fling with a guy, one of her lecturers. He wasn't married or anything like that; he was four or five years older than her. She'd liked him; she didn't think she'd loved him. It had been quite open. They'd held hands in public, around Belfield, a few times. She'd even met one of his old girlfriends in the student bar and they'd laughed about sharing him. She'd known it wasn't something that was going to last, and then she'd found out she was pregnant. He'd gone with her to London, her first time abroad. They'd gone across for four days. She'd had the abortion.

— No details, she said.

— Fine.

I remember saying it. I remember liking the way the word had sounded.

She'd liked London. It was why she'd moved there after she'd graduated. She'd been expected to do the H.Dip, and to go back home to teach.

— But you didn't.

— No.

— And now you're a TD.

— I'm resigning.

— Why?

— I shouldn't be doing it. I'm not the right — I don't believe in it.

She was going to go home at the weekend, and tell her family — her mother and her brother — about her decision and about the interview, and the abortion. Then she was going back to London. She was a Londoner, she said.

— I don't like this place, she said.

She meant the Government Buildings around the corner. She meant Dublin. She meant Ireland.

She stood up. She held out the newspaper she'd been reading when I'd arrived.

— Do you want it?

— No, thanks, I said.

— It was nice talking to you, she said.

She died five months later.

CHAPTER
SEVEN

I'd been coming to the pub later, making myself stay in the apartment a bit longer. I'd sit and force myself to write a page, sometimes two pages — I'd started five short stories. Then I'd go down to Donnelly's. I'd stare at one of the televisions — women's golf, Spanish football — and hope and dread that Fitzpatrick would come up behind me and slap my back. I'd seen him do that. I'd seen him in among other men, before he'd make his way across to me.

I didn't like him. I really didn't like him. He made me nervous. And he bored me. I hated it when he stood too close, or when he sat back, right in front of me, and scratched his crotch or walloped his stomach. And I couldn't remember him. He'd been in school with me; I didn't doubt that. But I couldn't see him when I thought about those years. He sometimes sat beside me in the pub and I tried to feel it, him beside me, to the left or to the right of me, forty years before. I saw myself sitting at a desk; I felt the heat of the room, or the cold; I saw the book — Irish, history, *Soundings* — open in front of me. I could remember, or assemble, those details. I could look around at faces I remembered, or just names. My memory was some sort of Brecht play; I was surrounded by surnames and nicknames scrawled on placards. Moonshine, Doc, Toner, Gaffney. Tom Jones, Patch, Super Cool. But never Fitzpatrick. He was in among the faceless. I didn't like him but I wanted to remember him. I wanted that bridge. Really, I wanted to be in among the men. To feel myself settle, to feel that — somehow — I was back.

There were some empty stools at the bar. I took one and waited for Carl. He was chatting and laughing with another barman. They were looking at something on Carl's phone. Then he saw me.

— Jesus, sorry.

— No problem.

— Your man here was distracting me. The usual?

I nodded.

— Cool, he said.

The Guinness tap was right in front of me.

— Summer's over, he said.

— Seems like it today.

— I stuck the gas fire on this morning for a bit, he said. — Didn't want to, but.

— You're getting old, I told him.

— Must be.

He was thirty or so, I guessed. Older than my son, but not much older. He had the beard and — I was guessing again — when he wasn't in his black work shirt, he wore plaid. I couldn't see any tattoos but I was betting there was a small one on his chest or on one of his legs.

He put the pint on the tray.

— You meeting your brother tonight? he asked.

— What?

— Are you meeting your brother?

— My brother?

— Is he not your brother?

— Who?

I sat up straighter so he could see me properly. He was mixing me up with someone else. His mind was still looking at whatever had been making him laugh a few minutes before.

— Sorry, he said. — I just thought you were brothers.

He had my pint back under the tap; he wanted to get out of this conversation.

— Who? I said. — Who's my brother?

I was smiling. I was safe here; I didn't have a brother.

— I just thought, he said. — I kind of took it for granted. The dude you're always with.

— Fitzpatrick?

— If that's his name, yeah.

If that was his name? Fitzpatrick was a regular; he'd been coming into this place for a long time before I'd arrived. I'd seen him in among the locals. I'd seen him looking at the women. I'd envied him.

— Ed, I said. — Fitzpatrick.

— Grand.

— He's not my brother.

— Cool, said Carl. — No offence. Here you go.

He lowered the pint in front of me. He hesitated — stopped before the glass made contact with the wood and flicked a beermat under it. I remember all this. He put the pint on the mat and waited a second before he took his hand away from the glass. I handed over the fiver.

— Thanking you, sir, he said.

The till was behind him.

— What made you think we were brothers? I asked his back.

— I don't know, really, he said.

— We're not alike, I said.

He turned and looked at me.

— No, he said. — No, you're not.

He put the change beside the pint. He looked along the bar to see if there was anyone wanting his attention. But it was still quiet.

— I've a brother, myself, he said. — Only a year and a bit between us. Actually, I've four brothers.

— Christ.

— And three sisters, he said. — A fuckin' madhouse, man. But this brother, the one nearest me. Darryl. We were ringers for each other when we were kids. We're not now, like. But when — up to about seventeen or eighteen or so. If he was here now, beside me here, you'd see we don't look like each other. But people who don't really know us still know we're brothers. When we're together, like.

He shrugged.

— That's all, he said. — That's all I meant. You seemed like brothers. The way when you're together.

— Okay, I said. — But we're not.

— Cool.

— We were in school together, I said.

— Oh — grand.

— Years ago.

— Cool, he said. — That might be it then. Being in school, like. Old buddies and that.

The place was filling. He left me alone.

CHAPTER
EIGHT

The interview with Aileen Clohessy was published six days before the referendum. A sitting TD, daughter of a junior minister in the Cosgrave coalition, a member of a party that was recommending that the country vote Yes for the rights of the unborn child, had revealed that she'd had an abortion. And she'd disappeared, back to England.

I was being claimed by both sides. I enjoyed the attention; I knew I was being talked about, and I liked it. I liked saying the word — *abortion*.

The first time I went into a radio studio, on a panel with four other people who'd clearly met and discussed tactics before I arrived, I said nothing. I didn't get a chance and I didn't really care. The presenter was covering for the regular tyrant and he was terrified of the man sitting to my right, Father Tom Prendergast.

Prendergast put his big — his huge — hand on my shoulder.

— I think it's great, he said, — young lads expressing their opinions.

His thumb went in under my collarbone. I was appalled, and then amused; this man who sang and laughed on *The Late Late Show*, behaving like a big thick in a schoolyard. He kept pressing until the green *on-air* light went on.

It wasn't that I said nothing of note that first time. I said nothing at all. The other four were veterans and buddies. The unborn were well looked after. But I wasn't cowed by Prendergast, or frightened. I was just raw. The presenter never asked me a question. He looked at me once during an ad break, and smiled.

But the fact that I was in the studio and referred to and thanked several times seemed to be enough. I was asked back. And I spoke. And caused outrage. I had to move out of my mother's house. Someone painted a cross on the front door and wrote "Killer" on the step with the rest of the red paint. One of the neighbours was helping my mother get the paint off when I came home.

— Look what you've caused, said Missis McCarthy.
— Yeh pup.

She was sweating and furious.

— What happened? I asked my mother.

— It's not too bad, she said. — It's coming off.

— It shouldn't've been put on in the first place, said Missis McCarthy. — Bastards.

They were both on their knees, side by side, facing the front door. The cross was gone but there was a smudge, a stain, where they hadn't been able to lift off all the paint. It wasn't red any more; it just looked like dirt.

I couldn't stay.

— The neighbours are grand, said my mother. — It wasn't anyone we know.

— How do you know, Mam?

— No one we know would do something like this, she said. — They'd have too much respect for your father.

She smiled; her eyes filled.

— Why did you have to talk about that, Victor?

— What?

— Abortion, love. Of all things.

— There was a referendum.

— And it's over, she said.

— The woman had an abortion, I said. — That's why I'm asked about it.

— You don't have to be there to answer them, she said.

— I thought you liked it.

— Not when you're talking about bloody abortion, she said.

— Do you think it's murder? I asked.

— Now he asks me, she said. — No. I don't. But I won't be jumping up and down telling people that.

— I'll go, I said.

I was earning money. I had the deposit; I'd have the rent at the end of every week. I liked the idea of being banished.

— You'll come and visit, she said.

— Of course.

She smiled. She cried.

— I am proud of you, she said.

— Thanks.

— So is Tilly.

She was talking about Missis McCarthy.

I took the record player and a lamp.

And I met Rachel. She sat down beside me outside a studio in RTE.

— You're the backstreet abortionist, she said, before I'd looked up from my book, *A Confederacy of Dunces*.

I looked at her.

— Aren't you? she said.

She was the most beautiful woman I had ever seen. I look at that sentence and I hate it. But it's honest. I gawked up at her — I must have been gawking.

— So, she said. — What are you in for?

— Round-up of the day's papers, I told her.

— You're not reading them, she said.

— I don't need to, I said.

She laughed.

I can still hear it.

— It's the same shite every day, I said.

We could hear the weather forecast — always a male voice back then — from the speaker above our heads. I was on next.

— What about you? I asked her.

Rachel was unusual thirty years ago. She's a national treasure now, but only because she was odd back then and had to fight. I think she was taken aback when I asked her why she was there. Taken aback, and pleased.

— My business, she said.

I thought she was telling me to mind my own.

— I'll be chatting about my business, she said.

— Oh.

— Yeah.

— What is it? I asked.

— It's boring, she said.

— What is it?

She laughed. She put two fingers on my arm.

— It's catering.

— Great, I said.

We felt the air shift to our right as the outer door to the studio opened.

— Victor, a jaded voice sighed from inside.

We grinned at each other; we knew we were better than this.

— Break a leg, she said.

— I probably will.

— Will you wait for me? she said. — After you're finished.

I couldn't believe what I'd heard. But I had to. It was the proof I'd needed. I'd become someone else.

— Yeah, I said. — Great.

That was the morning I announced that I was writing a book.

— Oh, ho, said the presenter, Myles Bradley. — We're in trouble, are we?

— You are, I said.

— What's it called, so?

— *Ireland*, I said. — *A Horror Story*.

— What's it about?

— Everything that's wrong about this country, I said.

— It's a pamphlet, said Bradley.

— A house brick.

— And packed full of our faults, is it?

— It will be.

— Good man, said Bradley. — We need a good bashing. That'll be a book worth waiting for, I'm sure.

— I hope so.

— Good man.

She drove me into town. She had a small, red van that smelled new, with *Meals on Heels* printed on its sides and back door, with a phone number.

— Great name, I said.

— Thanks.

I watched her feet on the pedals; she'd taken her shoes off. I watched her hands, her long fingers, gripping the wheel. I watched her put her black hair behind her ear. I watched her ear. I watched her mouth as she spoke and when she was waiting at the traffic lights. She only spoke when the van was moving.

— When will the book be out? she asked.

— When it's written, I said.

I had decided, before I got into the van: I wouldn't spoof, I wouldn't lie. I wouldn't embellish or diminish. I'd only come up with the title half an hour before but I was going to write the book. I was going home now to start. Because I was sitting beside her.

— What about you? I asked.

We were at traffic lights somewhere along Morehampton Road, so I watched the impact of the question on her before she answered. The impatience, the shoulders pushed slightly forward, willing the lights to get a move on — that stopped. The beautiful, comical twist at the side of her mouth changed direction, or shape. She was shocked, and delighted. For a second or two, I felt I was watching a nature programme, Attenborough whispering in my ear: *Note how the female responds when asked a question about herself.*

The lights turned green, and she shoved the van forward.

— What about me? she said.

— Your business, I said. — How does it work?

I'd heard her while I'd been waiting outside the studio. But Myles Bradley had spent most of the ten minutes flirting with her. *Here's a lovely lady and she's not going to be talking about fashion.* I'd heard her laughing, and I knew now that it wasn't her real laugh. I'd heard the real thing three or four times in the van, in the time it had taken us to get from Donnybrook to Leeson Street. Rachel laughed like a man. I don't mean she sounded like a man — Jesus, no. But she threw her head back, even in the car seat, and guffawed. She gave it the full "ha ha ha", not the "hee hee" she'd delivered when Bradley thought he was charming the tights off her in front of the nation.

— How does it work? she repeated my question.

— Yes, I said.

— Well, she said. — It's — You know when you're at a wedding?

— No, I said.

— You've never been to a wedding?

— No, I said. — Not yet.

She grinned.

— Really?

I thought I'd got away with it. She'd missed "Not yet". But she hadn't, she told me later. She'd thought I was stupid, sweet and lovely.

— Really, I said. — Never been to one. Funerals are my speciality.

— Well then, she said. — You're given a choice of maybe two main courses. Usually fucking chicken.

I was in love.

— But, she said, — we allow the client to have an open choice. We don't give them a list or a menu. We let them make their own menu.

— Who's "we"? I asked.

She laughed. She knew I was already jealous.

— Well, she said. — "We" is actually me. I was told I'd sound less like a psycho or a ruthless bitch if I said "we" instead of "me" or "I".

— Who told you that? I asked.

— My father.

— Oh.

— He's a prick, my dad, she said. — But it makes sense. "We" says it's a bigger operation than it actually is at the moment, and that it's backed by more experience. "We" says I'm not just a little girl playing recipes in the kitchen. And I can hide behind it.

But she didn't.

— So "we" is me for now, and I've a pool of girls who I can call on when I need them.

— Do you do weddings? I asked.

— No, she said. — Women prefer to be told what to do when it comes to their weddings. Their mothers become involved.

— Mothers are bad, yeah?

— God, yes. A fucking nightmare.

She laughed again, head back, as we chugged out onto Stephen's Green.

— What about you? she said. — What's your mum like?

— Great.

— Boy's answer, she said.

I laughed. I know now: I didn't laugh much until I met Rachel. It's corny but true. I only laughed when other people were laughing. But now I started laughing. I *started* laughing, and she joined me.

She stopped outside the Unitarian Church.

— Well, she said.

— Well.

— Are we going to see each other again?

— Where are you going now? I said. — I'll give you hand if you want.

She laughed.

Rachel doesn't laugh on TV. I love that about her. She's always kept that back. No one who doesn't know her knows that Rachel laughs.

— You'd better get home, she said. — And finish your book.

She was looking straight at me.

— Or start your book.

Last time: she laughed.

There was once — this was just after we'd moved in together — we were still fucking long after the music had stopped. It was early evening, some midweek day. Our metal-framed windows, a line of them right along the long wall, were all open. The odd shout, the odd car horn and bus braking, the tick-tick of the needle waiting to be lifted off the record, our grunts — these

94

were the sounds. Grunts — I'd stopped saying anything long before. Rachel too — nothing like a word had passed her lips. She was on her back, on the mattress — half on the mattress. Her legs were wrapped around me, up at my shoulders, and her fingers were on my back, my arse. I cried out. It was the roar of an animal and I loved it. Later. I could make this sound; it was in me. I owned it. And I owned it because the woman beneath me, the grunting, sweating animal that was pushing herself against me, had given it to me.

— Jesus Christ, she said when we separated and I lay back beside her. — Jesus Christ.

We lay there, taking our breath back.

— You must have finished a chapter today, did you? she said.

— Nearly, I said.

— Well, give me a call when you actually do finish it, she said. — I want another of those.

— How was *your* day?

— Not as good as yours, she said. — Until now.

That still makes me happy.

She loved the mess.

— Oh, yeuk!

She loved it when we were glued together. She loved backing into me. She loved making me groan. She loved groaning.

She loved me. I never doubted that — she didn't let me. She still says she loves me and I believe her. Then, it filled me. Later, it made me want to lie down on the ground, in public. It made me want to kill her.

But then. Then. She made me work, she made me want to work; she made me believe in what I was doing or bracing myself to do. She really did. I can just about remember that; I can just about feel it. I wanted Rachel to be proud of me. I remember too, I wanted to deserve my sex. She had nothing to gain from me. She saw the face of a besotted man who was no good to her whatsoever. There was no advantage in letting me kiss her tits, in letting me share her nights and early mornings. And she loved me for it. She saw a man who loved her. Who loved looking at her. Being with her. Touching her, feeling her. Thinking about her. Who grinned when he saw her. Loved her.

It hadn't started that way. There'd been no glue.

We'd agreed to meet in Kehoe's on South Anne Street that first time. But as I walked up to the pub, I saw her standing outside, in the lane off the street. She had her back to the wall, and one foot. The foot was tapping the wall as if to music, although there was none. She was wearing a short black skirt and black boots, and a coat that I now know was charcoal. I was five minutes late and I panicked; I thought I'd fucked up. It was anger that was making her foot tap; she was going to give me the push.

She shoved herself away from the wall with her foot. Then she was walking towards me, meeting me.

— Hi.

— Sorry I'm late.

— No.

Her face kept coming. She was going to kiss me. I was going to have to kiss her. Her lips landed on mine.

She was looking straight at me. She pushed me back slightly — with her lips — then stepped back, herself. One step.

— Hi, she said again.

— Hi, I said. — Will we go in?

— Yes — okay.

— Why didn't you wait inside?

— Too much hassle, she said.

— What d'you mean?

I was holding the door for her. I'd remembered my manners.

— Thank you, sir.

And I knew I'd asked a stupid question. Every man in the house was staring at her, even the seven dwarfs, the scabby-headed little men who worked behind Kehoe's bar. I was the only man in the shop not looking at her. We went down to the room at the back and people squashed to give us room — to give *her* room. I went out to the bar and she was chatting to a gang of people when I came back in with our pints. Rachel drank pints of Guinness. She was listening to another girl — woman — nodding her head, putting her hair back behind her ear so she could catch the words, and I thought I'd lost my chance. She'd found better company. The guy beside the girl was looking at Rachel. He wasn't a guy; he was a man. He wasn't older but he looked it, somehow. Because he stayed still, because he was wearing a black coat. Because he looked like he could have been living in any decade. I found room for the pints on the Formica table and sat beside, dropped myself beside Rachel. And she turned to me. Our legs, my right, her left, were pressed against each other. She shifted slightly so she was leaning into me and I watched her drink for the first time. Her leg, her shoulder, her breast were pressing against me and now her chin almost touched mine while she knocked back a fifth of her pint, leaned out and put the glass back down on the table, and came back up to me.

— So, she said. — This is nice.

I almost resented it. She was so physically there, right up against me. It was too much. I'd have been happier sitting there watching her chat to the woman and watching the man watch her. I'd have been happier feeling left out. It would have been normal.

— What's your favourite film? she said.

And we started to talk. She knew a stupid question would get us going. And it did. We moved from films to music and books and back to films and the rest of the world wasn't there for a while, until it was her turn to get the pints and I watched her being watched and I felt proprietorial and lost. She'd keep walking, even though her coat was right beside me. She'd keep going, out the door. I was a clown and she'd give up the coat to get away from me. But I knew she'd be back and I knew we'd keep going and we wouldn't be going our separate ways at closing time. I'd have to be careful. I wasn't a good drinker and she clearly was. I didn't really get drunk; I just got filled. A bit stupid, and slow. I staggered sometimes, missed corners, mumbled when I was by myself. But I didn't sing or howl. I didn't become clever or brave. I just headed towards sleep. I was a waste of money. She, I knew, wouldn't be like that. She'd be a bit mad. She'd be looking at me, waiting for a response, a riposte, and I'd be wiping my chin and working hard at keeping my eyes wide open. She came back with two pints and got to her place, past me. I could have shifted, to make room for her, or let her take the space I'd been taking and I'd take hers. But I didn't. I was inflexible — still am. I loosened a bit, for her, but it was always a fight. My place was mine; hers was hers. I like order. She bent her leg so she could get past my knees without toppling the table. Her arse was hovering over my lap. She got past me and sat and faced me again, and smiled.

—Where were we?

The pub disappeared and the only thing there was her face — and all of her. Two pints — two interruptions — later, she announced that she was moving on.

—Want to come to a party?

I hated parties, hated arriving, walking into the hall, the room, the shit music — it was always shit. Soft Cell, Jimmy Somerville, Pat Benatar. Love Is a fuckin' Battlefield. I hated knowing I'd be leaving alone. I hated walking home, along the Stillorgan Road or Clontarf Road or Appian Way at five in the morning, hating that I didn't know how to enjoy myself, hating the girl who'd smiled at me, hating myself for not crossing the room, hating myself for surrendering yet again, that this time it would be different, that I'd lighten up, I'd make the move, rejection wouldn't destroy me. Fuckin' idiots had parties, fuckin' idiots went to them.

— Sure, I said.

— Cool.

She followed me out to the lane, and back onto South Anne Street. I had my hands in the pockets of my army surplus coat. Her hand, her arm, went between my right arm and side and into my pocket and around my hand. It was the best thing that had ever happened to me. I don't remember much about the party, whose it was or where it was. I don't think we took off our coats. I don't recall putting a bottle to my mouth. I do remember going out to the back garden for a piss. I remember a voice beside me.

— Is this where the big nobs hang out?

It was a guy I could hardly see. I heard him pissing onto the flowerbed a few yards away from where I was still pissing. I don't remember going back in but I do remember the terror at not being able to find her, and I remember that because it was how I always felt, even today. But I found her and we kissed.

I forgot: she smoked. It was what I tasted when my tongue was in her mouth. And it didn't matter. I couldn't believe it, couldn't quite accept it, when her mouth was open and her tongue was nudging mine. I had my hands on her back, beneath her coat, my fingers on — in — the canyon that ran along her spine. She took her tongue from my mouth — I was kind of relieved — and rested her forehead on mine. My eyes were swimming but I could see her smile. She was talking to someone beside me.

— Great, thanks; fab. No, yes — that's just bizarre. Yeah, next week.

100

We were pressed into each other, and she pushed a bit more, rubbed her stomach against me. She moaned; she let me hear it.

— I live near here, she said.

—Yeah?

— But we can't go there.

The way she said it, I wasn't to be disappointed. She had her hand in one of my back pockets.

—Why not?

— My dad would go mad.

—Yeah?

— Oh yeah.

—What about your mother?

— She wouldn't notice.

— Really?

— No, she would. She wouldn't be angry, if — you know. She found us in the kitchen. But she wouldn't talk to me for years.

—Years?

— Months. Weeks. No, yeah — years.

She squeezed my arse. We kissed again. I took my mouth away.

— My dad wouldn't object, I said.

— Really?

— He's dead.

— Not funny.

— He is.

She didn't take her forehead from mine. I can't remember what song was playing, just that it was shit.

—What about your mum?

— I don't live with her, I told her.

— Ah, she said. — Bingo.

She pulled me even closer to her. She spoke right into my ear.

— Let's go.

But she disappeared. She'd stopped holding me. She'd left the room. I stayed where I was. I wiped my mouth. I buttoned my coat. I waited; I thought I was waiting — I wasn't sure now. I tried to remember where we were, and how best to get to my flat. But she didn't come back. I went to the door, looked out at the hall. The house was huge; the hall was packed and cold. There was a smell of dope, even though the front door was wide open. There was some sort of a row going on, someone being thrown out. Was she outside waiting for me? Was she with someone else in a room upstairs? I remember thinking, wondering — my excitement curling into something painful in my gut. What sort of an idiot was I? How had I got all the messages wrong? I'd go, I decided — when she was suddenly beside me.

— Ready?

— Yeah.

I followed her through the crowd, to the front door. She knew everyone — she seemed to. But I'd learn, I'd slowly realise: Rachel had no friends. Except me. But I had none either. I'd got rid of them all. I'd drifted away from my old life, from the lads I'd grown up with, friends — boys I'd loved and hated, woken up thinking about. I'd kept in touch with no one. Rachel was different. She was bang in the middle of her habitat. She'd known the people at the party all her life. She'd gone to school with some, college with others. There were cousins here, and men she'd slept with. They all liked her and she smiled at all of them as she led me out. But none of them were friends. She was alone. I didn't know this at the time. I was just following her, a bit terrified.

She was walking stiffly; it wasn't her usual walk.

Rachel's walk. My mother told me that Rachel walked like a Protestant. I saw a similar walk years later, in *House of Cards*. Claire Underwood walked like Rachel. Or, if Claire Underwood had grown up in a place where you were often trying to get out of the rain, she'd have walked like Rachel. Rachel never wore heels but that was always a surprise. She never strolled. She was always going from A to B. But Christ. She — it; her walk — was fuckin' wonderful. There was nothing angelic or ghostly about it; Rachel was human. She strode and she sometimes whistled.

But as I followed her out of the house she was lopsided and, once we were out on the street, I knew why.

— Ta-dah! Look what I've got.

She had a bottle of wine hidden under her coat. And a corkscrew in one of her pockets.

— The only one in the house, she said. — I think.

I followed her around a corner, to a wider, even more tree-lined street. She put the bottle on a wall and began to attack the cork.

— Come on, little cork — yes!

She threw the corkscrew into a hedge and put the bottle to her mouth. She gulped it like a pint, then wiped the neck and passed it to me. I pretended to swallow more than I actually did. I wasn't trying to stay sober. I wasn't being evil. I just didn't want to get sick. My act must have worked because she put her hand on the bottle and waited for me to release it.

— Shouldn't have thrown the cork away, she said. — Stupid fucking me. Ah well.

She walked. I followed, caught up. She put her arm through mine.

— Where? she said.

— I'm not sure. Where are we?

— Blackrock.

— Rathmines, I said. — How do we get there?

She put her mouth to mine, held on to my coat with the hand not holding the bottle, as if we were both standing on a deck during a storm — we swayed together — and she kissed me.

She let go.

— We could do with a taxi, she said.

And one came around the corner. Empty taxis were as rare as giraffes but a taxi turned the corner, Rachel stepped out onto the road and it stopped. We climbed into the back and Rachel nudged me once, twice, until I gave the driver my address. She drank from the bottle as we went, and I tried not to. We got up to my flat and out of our clothes. I fell over but landed on the bed. She followed me. The wine bottle hit the side of my head. She was still holding it. She'd managed to get undressed without letting go of the bottle. She didn't apologise. She didn't notice. I didn't either, really. I'd heard the bump but I hadn't felt it. All I knew was that I didn't have an erection. And I knew there wouldn't be one. And I knew I could blame the drink. I remember her skin. The smoothness of it, the impossibility of it, the heat. We were on our knees, swaying on the bed. I heard her put the bottle on the floor beside it; she pushed some books out of the way. She leaned across to do it. I rubbed her back. She pushed herself back a bit, put one hand on my hip and my cock in her mouth. And nothing happened. I wanted it to stop. I wanted to get off the bed and put on a record. I could hear her but I couldn't feel a thing. There was nothing there.

It had happened before. It had happened — not happened — every time. I'd never had sex. I'd never penetrated a woman. I'd known that on the way up the stairs, while I got my clothes off, while I sent my hands over her skin.

She stopped.

— Sorry, I said.

She said nothing back. She lay down on the bed. I stayed where I'd been, kneeling beside her, hoping that, now that she'd gone, my blood would rush to my penis. I put my hand around it, gave it a tug, tried to bully it.

— Lie down here, she said.

She was talking to the wall. Her back was to my knees. I got down beside her. I covered us with the clean sheet I'd put on the bed that afternoon; I'd bought the sheets two days before in BHS. I covered us up. I placed my hand on her waist and kept it going until it rested on her stomach. She was so warm. Her hot arse rested in my lap and her hand took mine. She lifted it off her stomach and brought it to her right breast and left her own hand on top of it. I knew then it was fine. I knew she'd stay with me for a while. She fell asleep before I did. I fell asleep with my hand still on her breast. She was still there, exactly there, when I woke. She was still asleep. There was early daylight on the other side of the curtain. I lifted the blankets carefully, so I could look at her and believe that she was there.

We were drunk again the second time. We were cold and wet and we dived in under the blankets. I didn't mind being naked; I wasn't embarrassed. She put my hand between her legs. She started to shake, to quiver. I felt her wet hair on my chest as she lifted herself off me and grabbed my arm at the same time. I didn't know what was happening — I did; I had a fair idea. She was crying. I was bright enough not to stop and ask her if she was alright. I knew she was alright. I knew she was coming. I knew I'd done my job, somehow. I knew there'd be a next time. Because she lay down again beside me. She pushed herself gently back, and found her parking space. She was humming just one note. Her hair was wet and cold, her arse was hot. I kissed her back. She moaned. I kissed again. She pressed gently, and moaned. She found my hand again and put it on her tit. She went to sleep.

The third time, I came on her hand. She rubbed her palm across my chest and kissed it.

The fourth time, I let her see my erection.

— Oh fuck, I said. — Oh, fuck, oh fuck, oh fuck.

I discovered something. Words in her ear — she loved them. They actually lifted her off the bed. Any words, but especially filth, biological facts, the fuckin' obvious

106

— *I'm going to come, I'm going to come* — they worked like fingers. She'd be lost in her explosion, right under me. I was overjoyed, the happiest, the biggest man on earth, listening in and trying not to laugh until she did. And she always did laugh. She came down from the madness, stretched her full length and guffawed. Her hand found mine and she brought it to her tit.

— Wake me if you want another seeing to.

And she always fell asleep before me.

CHAPTER
NINE

One hand was all he needed to hold me down. A hand on my back, just above my hips. I was helpless. He didn't have to press too hard; he knew exactly what he was doing. I gave up trying to lift myself. I could see his shoes and black socks. The socks were weird, nearly see-through, like tights. I could see under the desk, and the bottom of the door on the other side. It was getting dark outside, and the room was dark.

— Now, he said. — Now.

He wasn't angry. He'd no reason to be. He'd told me to come to the room after last class. He was going to teach me how to wrestle. He was going to teach me how to protect myself. He knew my father was sick and back in hospital. He'd asked me how my father was just before he told me to come at him like I was going to attack.

— Come on now, Victor, he said. — Don't be shy. You want to kill me.

I got it over with. I walked towards him, and right up to him. He flipped me around before I knew he'd grabbed me, and he dumped me on the carpet. It knocked the air out of me but I wasn't hurt. My face hadn't hit the floor.

— Now, he said again.

I heard him getting his breath back. I thought he might be shivering. I could feel it in his hand and arm — I thought I could.

— Did you see how I did that? he said.

I couldn't answer. It was like he was holding my voice down with his hand too. I couldn't speak. My face was a few inches from the waste basket.

— Well? he said.

His other hand rubbed my leg, from behind the knee up towards my arse. I couldn't move. I couldn't try to. His hand went to my other leg.

— You can do that with anyone, he said. — It doesn't matter what size they are. That's why I'm teaching you now. Any gutty that comes near you, you'll be able to deal with him.

He'd reached the fork in my jeans. He pushed his fingers, his palm, under me. He held me there — just held me.

— Now, he said. — We'll do it again. And then we'll see if you can do it to me.

His hands were gone.

— Up you get.

— Thank you, Brother.

CHAPTER
TEN

She'd call the payphone and I usually made it down the stairs before the man in the room beside the front door got to it. He'd often watch me from his door as I talked to her.

— Was that Rachel, Victor? he asked me once after I'd put the phone down.

— It was, Oscar.

— She sounds very nice, he said.

— Thanks, I said. — She is.

He was too old for a one-room bedsit, I thought. (The young are so fuckin' stupid.) He was a kitchen porter and didn't work on Mondays. Six pairs of checked trousers hung from the clothesline in the back garden every Monday afternoon. Rachel saw them from my window.

— Oh, look, she said. — I wear those too.

She did, and she didn't. She could have gone out and taken a pair off the line and put them on. I could see her down there, in the drizzle, lifting a leg, then the other, wriggling till her arse and hips had made it past the soggy waist of Oscar's work trousers and, yes, laughing while she did it. But Rachel's trousers were

110

different. She wore them the next time she came to my place. She made me take them off.

She stayed a few nights a week. We fucked like happy rabbits and she cooked glorious meals, created from the nothing in my fridge.

— How did you do that? I asked.

Our plates were on our laps as we ate side by side on my single bed.

— Do what?

— Make this.

I tapped the plate.

— Well, she said. — You had two tomatoes and I smuggled the rest in in my bag.

— You didn't bring a bag, I said. — I didn't see one.

She'd shown me the spare pair of knickers she'd brought in her jacket pocket and she already had a toothbrush parked beside mine above the triangular sink in the corner, beside the cooker.

— I've been sneaking ingredients in for weeks, she said. — Did you not notice?

— No.

I looked across at the shelf above the sink. There were three slim bottles staring back at me.

— Spices, I said.

— Yes.

— Three kinds.

— Yes.

— Jesus.

I didn't tell her that I must have been staring at them every time I pissed in the sink on the nights when she wasn't there. But I hadn't seen them.

— What's this stuff? I asked her.

— Couscous.

— It's good.

It wasn't on the shelf.

— Where's it hidden?

— I'm not telling you, she said.

I was eating a thing called couscous and there were no peas or spuds on the plate, or meat. I was doing this as I sat beside a naked woman. There was a mug of wine on the floor beside me. I felt French. I felt American. I felt like a writer, living the writer's life. I felt handsome. I felt cruel and good, adult and giddy. I felt sophisticated, and I didn't. I felt that this was mine. My life had started. My real life had started.

I sat for hours at the table in my room and filled pages, so there'd be evidence there the next time she stayed. I wrote pieces for *What Now* and the *Sunday Independent*, so she'd see my name. I went on *The Late Late Show*, as part of a panel of "young people", so she'd see me. That was the difference between us. I worked for her approval but Rachel didn't work for mine. I filled pages because she wanted me to. I bought an Olivetti typewriter, so she'd hear me working as she came up the stairs after Oscar had let her in.

— She's a beautiful girl, Victor.

— She is, Oscar.

— She's got a lovely smile.

— Yes.

— She was wearing chef trousers.

— That's right.

— She's a chef.

— She is.

I'd type for hours, knowing — hoping — she'd hear me on her way up. I'd run across to the kettle but I'd charge back to make sure she'd hear me being a writer. I'd try to look surprised when I opened the door.

— Sorry, I'd say. — I was miles away.

She brought a cassette to the bedsit. She had it in a bag. The bag was pink and plastic, with *Meals on Heels* and a tray on two stiletto heels printed on its side. If a tray could be sexy, this one was. The bags became well known, and sought after, but this one was brand new. She took the cassette from the bag and dropped it, the bag, on the floor. She hadn't said hello or kissed me.

— What's wrong?

— Nothing.

She took a Dylan bootleg from the player on the mantelpiece and put in her cassette.

— This is my father's favourite piece of music, she said.

It was violins and cellos. I knew nothing about classical music.

— What is it? I asked.

— Samuel Barber's *Adagio for* fucking *Strings*, she said.

And she fucked me. She pulled me to the floor by the sleeve of my jumper. Then she kneeled in front of me — she wasn't smiling. She turned her back and dropped onto her elbows. She was wearing a black skirt and her right hand came back and grabbed the hem. She lifted it slowly. *Adagio for Strings* is well known now; we've seen Willem Dafoe dying to it. But Rachel was lifting her skirt two or three years before *Platoon* was released. She backed into me and she kept backing into me, shoving herself right through me, long after I'd come and Barber had gone, replaced by some header with a piano.

— Who the fuck is that?

— Liszt.

She'd let herself fall forward and I was lying on top of her, sweating, elated, devastated. The *Adagio* had almost made me cry and that now made me want to laugh. She groaned. It wasn't an objection; she wanted me to stay where I was. I rested my cheek on the back of her neck. She lifted a hand, and managed to find my other cheek and pat it.

— I love you, I said.

I couldn't believe what I'd just done. I seemed to hear each word and my voice, the horsey whisper of a well-fucked young man, seconds after I'd spoken. I'd wrecked it; I'd fuckin' wrecked it. I wanted to get up off her, and out of the room.

I could feel her breathing; she was lifting me with each inhalation, and dropping me when she exhaled. My sweat was cold — my knees were killing me. My mouth was open; I think I was trying to catch the words, grab them back. I wanted to cry again.

There was a delay — it was a delay. She was going to speak now.

— That's nice, she said.

She meant it, I was sure; there was no sarcasm. (She told me she loved me too about eight months later.)

Her bum nudged me.

— Lift.

I got off her. My arms were trembling. I began to stand up.

— No, she said.

She turned on her side and stayed there. She pulled her hair from her face. She was smiling. I lay beside her. She leaned out and kissed me.

— My man, she said.

She took my hand and brought it down to her fanny.

— Finish me off, she said.

She grinned and licked my ear.

— Hang on, I said.

I got up on my knees, so I could reach up to the cassette player. I walked my finger across the top, to the Stop button. I pushed it. The piano stopped dead just as her fingers touched my balls.

She stopped.

— Will I switch it back on? I said.

She laughed, and I lay back down on the strange blue carpet and we hugged and she came just as my wrist was about to break, and she gripped me like she thought she was falling off a roof. Her fingers hurt me. They left bruises that later, when I examined them, made me happy.

— What's for dinner? I said.

She bit my arm.

— You.

I pretended she'd hurt me and pushed myself away. She followed me like I'd hoped she would. I was lying on the pink *Meals on Heels* bag. I pulled it out from under me.

— This is nice.

— Dad's little present. I fucking hate it.

— Oh.

Adagio for Strings began to make sense.

— I have five thousand of them, she said. — As of this afternoon.

— Maybe he means well, I said. — Does he?

— No.

— No?

She didn't repeat herself. She put me in her mouth and I managed to hold off coming in time to grab the *Meals on Heels* bag, flick it open, lift her head from me, and come into the bag.

She clapped her hands.

— Oh Jesus — amazing.

She laughed till the walls sweated. She watched as I went the few steps to the waste bin under the table and pushed the bag down into it, on top of the paper I'd crumpled and thrown in there, to prove that I was working.

— I'll never be able to use them now, she said.

But she did.

— What's the problem with them? I asked.

— They're fucking pink, for a start. Have you ever seen me wear anything pink?

I was on safe ground.

— No.

— Or even lean against anything pink?

— No.

— It's none of his business, she said. — He doesn't trust me. I'm only a girl and girls are for marrying. And

116

the heels — he made the whole thing look pornographic.

— A pornographic tray?

— Yes, Victor. Pornographic anything.

She stood up.

— He went guarantor for my loan and he thinks that makes him the boss. Or the boss's boss, or something.

The curtains were open but my room was at the back of the house, two flights up. Someone at the very back of the garden could have seen her, or anyone cutting the grass or playing with the kids in the gardens on the other side of the back wall. I was happy to share her. I was happy to gloat. She rubbed and slapped dust and grit from her legs and back and shoulders.

— You're a damn fine woman, I said.

She was dusting her knees. She looked at me, through her hair. She smiled; she was pleased. She was happy.

— I am, she said. — Aren't I?

— Yes, you are.

— I'm a woman, she said.

— Eh — yes.

I was happy too. I had my woman here. I was in love — overwhelmed. I liked myself too, I think. I even liked her father until I met him.

I brought her to meet my mother first, on a Sunday afternoon, after we'd gone for a walk in Howth.

— My God, Victor, my mother whispered when Rachel went upstairs to the toilet. — Is she a Protestant?

— No.

— She's beautiful — her teeth. She's beautiful.

My mother looked at me. She grinned — she giggled. She stopped and put her hand on my arm. My life made complete sense to her now. She'd just seen its measure going up the stairs. I never had to explain myself again.

She dusted the kettle before she filled it.

— Not in here, she said.

We were in the kitchen.

— The front room, she said. — Go on. Grab her before she comes in here.

—What's wrong with here?

— Ah, Victor.

She'd taken three clean cups from the cupboard and now she was washing them. She looked back at me.

— I'll only be a minute, she said.

But she was still smiling.

— Go on, she said. — Do what you're told for once. There's the flush, listen. Head her off at the pass — go on.

I caught Rachel at the bottom of the stairs. She looked too bright for the house, although she was wearing black — black dress and tights, black boots. Her charcoal coat was hanging at the door, beside my mother's raincoat and my sister's grey school blazer. She looked too bright and too big.

— I've to bring you in here, I told her.

I tried to be light. I was making my mother happy and that made me happy. But I was embarrassed. The smallness of the room, and the cold in there; it was hardly ever used. The narrowness of the hall, the wallpaper, the little boy on the wall with the big tearful eyes, the line of porcelain cats, even the photograph of my father. They — *it* — embarrassed me. I had to swallow back the apology. I knew how it would sound but it was still a fight.

Rachel timed it perfectly. My mother came in with the tray just as she picked up the photograph of my father.

— He's gorgeous, she said.

— Yes, he was, said my mother. — He was a good-looking man.

She put the tray down on the glass coffee table. There was a rattle of cups and spoons. She stood beside Rachel and they looked at my father together.

— Like Victor, said Rachel.

My mother patted Rachel's arm and Rachel put the photograph back on the mantelpiece.

—You must miss him, said Rachel.

—You've no idea, love, said my mother.

They were both at the tray, bent over, and I felt I didn't know them. How had Rachel known to say something like that? And my mother's answer had been almost vicious, a sharpness to her voice that I'd never heard — or noticed — before. And yet what they'd said had been perfect. They were friends and, somehow, they were ganging up on me. Rachel had smelled my embarrassment and she was siding with my mother. *She gets down on her hands and knees*, I wanted to tell my mother. *She makes me fuck her from behind.* But I

119

could hear my new mother. *Good for her*, she'd say. *Good for her*.

I was tempted to go up to my old room, to leave them alone, get away for a bit. But I didn't. I knew Rachel would have followed me and I didn't want her to see it — although she might have had a peek already when she was upstairs. I didn't want her to see the Derby County poster or the absence of a headboard on my bed, or the damp patch and the corner of peeling wallpaper over the window, or the view from the window of O'Connells' back garden and the craters dug in the grass by their Alsatian. The dog was dead but the holes were still there, and a broken Honda 50 on its side. I didn't want her to hear Mister and Missis O'Connell riding, bashing each other against the wall, like they did every Sunday afternoon. And yet, I did. I wanted her to see and hear it all. I knew she'd love it. She'd think it was great that old people fucked and didn't care about their garden. She'd sit on the bed and smile at me. I was protecting myself, not Rachel. Rachel was never a snob. But she didn't have to be. I did.

But I loved my mother. I don't know if I loved my father. I don't remember him dying. I remember him being dead and I remember being in the graveyard. I remember being cold. I remember not knowing how to feel, what to do. I loved my mother and that was why I'd brought Rachel to the house. To show her off, and to make my mother happy. To let my mother know that I'd grown up; I was a man. To let her see that I'd gone

120

up in the world and that she mightn't be seeing that much of me any more.

I hadn't expected them to get on so well. They were best buddies, giddy sisters. My mother loved the way Rachel ate the plate of Goldgrain biscuits. She marvelled at it, this walking proof of female perfection chewing and slurping, and throwing her head back whenever my mother said something funny. My mother *was* funny!

She offered my mother a job.

— You'd be perfect, she said.

— Ah no.

My mother was forty-five. I've just worked that out and it's a shock. She was a young woman. She was good-looking. It was Sunday and she was still in her mass clothes. The slippers she'd been wearing when she'd let us into the house were gone, replaced by the black high heels she wore once a week. This is me, now, looking back. But then, I didn't see the woman I now know was there. I saw the lines at the eyes, the protruding tummy, the too-black hair, the nicotine-stained fingers. I wanted her to be different.

And I didn't.

— I couldn't cope with that, she told Rachel. — I'd drop the bloody tray, sure.

— You wouldn't.

— Oh, I would. Sure, I nearly toppled this one here just now. Anyway, I have a job and I'm grand with it.

I'd already told Rachel; my mother cleaned offices. She got the bus into town every workday evening with a gang of her neighbours.

— I like the company, she told Rachel.

—You'd have company with me too, said Rachel.

—Yes, said my mother.

She laughed.

—Young ones like you, she said. — Gorgeous.

She patted Rachel's arm.

— I'm happier with girls my own age, she said. — I can hold my own in the middle of them. But I'd look like a bloody banshee beside your ones.

— Banshees are cool.

—They are in their eye, love. I've heard them often enough.

She patted Rachel's arm again and looked across at me. She was smiling, almost tearful.

— My God, she said.

Rachel had moved in with me. She wouldn't live in the same house as her father any more. We fucked till we were starving. But it was awkward. It was only one room — two windows, two chairs, one table, one single, sagging bed. The typewriter had to be shifted if we were going to eat at the table. I had to add new pages every day to the pile beside the typewriter. I had to let her see that the book was growing. I got a key cut for her and I didn't bother telling the landlord; I knew we wouldn't be staying. We needed somewhere bigger — a shower of our own, a toilet, a proper cooker, a bed made for two. I needed an office to hide in.

I loved falling asleep against her. I loved the smell in the room. I loved watching her move, any movement at all, her steps across to the tap or just scratching her ankle. She saw me watching, and smiled.

— What?

We put the telly on the floor beside the bed and lay on our sides, watching *Remington Steele*. I was behind Rachel, with my chin on her shoulder. The ads came on. Rachel leaned out and turned down the sound. She let herself fall back, and felt my erection tapping her.

— Oh dear.

She kicked off the sheet, lifted her left leg high and put me inside her.

— Quick, before Pierce comes back.

She loved *Remington Steele*, one woman's cheerful fight against male domination and Pierce Brosnan. We were kind of proud of Pierce, an Irishman holding his own in the middle of all that Americanness. That was where we were headed, I thought. America, or at least a bigger place. We were publicly together now, the gorgeous young businesswoman and the pup who kept shocking the nation by saying words like "condoms" and "atheist".

But we were photographed just once before the loft, for the *Sunday Independent*. We were in an apartment that Rachel borrowed for the afternoon from a school friend's mother. Dalkey Island was behind us. Rachel wore black, including the apron. I refused to dress up; I tried to look like I'd been hauled from my study. I refused to look at the camera. I even held some sheets of A4 paper. In the shot they used, I stared at a page — it was blank — while Rachel leaned against me and

123

pointed at an invisible sentence with a white plastic spatula.

— Interesting, she whispered.

— Spatula, I whispered back.

She'd told me what it was called just a minute before. We helped the photographer and his assistant pack the gear; we bullied them out the door. Then we fucked for the half-hour we had before the school friend's mammy came home. Rachel picked up the blank pages and looked at them.

— No work done today, Victor. You have been a naughty boy.

She sat back on the leather couch — she looked quite small on it — and patted her knees. I lay over her and she whacked me on the arse with her spatula.

— For fuck sake, Rachel!

She pressed an elbow into my back to hold me down, and whacked again. I broke away. *Come on, Victor, don't be shy, you want to kill me.* I pushed her elbow aside, and stood.

— That hurt!

— So fuck me, she said.

She took my anger and made me laugh. The glory of it — her legs around me. Me. I don't think I ever quite believed it. Or accepted it.

The drum kit was a surprise. I hadn't known about the boy in the house. I knew about Rachel's sisters and I'd been looking forward to having a gawk at them, and I'd been dreading it too. But she hadn't told me anything about a brother.

124

There wasn't one.

— It's his, she told me quietly.

— Whose?

— Dad's.

— Your da plays the drums?

— No, she said. — Not really. He just owns them.

We'd come into the house through the back door. The kitchen was empty, and that was weird. The smells were right but I don't think I'd been in an empty kitchen in daylight before. It wasn't the room where the living was done. The door to the rest of the house was shut.

Rachel opened it.

— Hi!

We stood in the hall. Tiles, rugs, dark tables, seven shut doors, a wide stairs, and the drum kit. A door opened to my left, then another to my right. In five or six seconds, I was facing Rachel's family. They'd all come from different directions. A sister — Maeve — was first, a ringer for Rachel, except not. She was too tall, too toothy, too nearly like Rachel. Then there was the mother. She was drunk. I wasn't used to observing the efforts of people who drank secretly. But I knew. It was the deliberate quality of every move. She opened the door — *her* door, then shut the door. Then she looked and smiled, at Rachel, at me, at Maeve, at Rachel again. Then she spoke.

— Well, hello.

Well — hello.

Then she moved. She took the edge of the rug like Becher's Brook; she didn't trip or lunge.

— You must be Victor.

You — mustbe — Victor.

— This is Mum.

She shook my hand and reminded herself to let go. She was doing very well.

Then the other sister. Esther. This one was older, and angry. She carried a book like it was a hammer.

— So, she said, and stared at me.

She wanted to fight. She wanted me to lean out and push her, so she could push me back. We'd grab each other and throw ourselves onto the drums. She'd beat my face to mush with her hardback copy of *Lord of the Rings*.

Then came Dad. Everything about him said rugby player. Everything about him said rugby player who had not been good enough. Rugby player who had never been any good. Rugby player who would take it out on the world with a smile on his square face until he exploded and died. He stood in front of me, beside his wife. She was pissed and slightly sideways but she was the nearest thing to Rachel in the hall. He was protecting her. *She's mine — I used to fuck her, she feeds me.* And he smiled. *I'm going to pound you and then I'm going to shove you under the rug with the side of my foot.*

— The notorious Victor, he said.

— Hello, Mister Carey.

— Jim.

It was a threat, a verb. He was going to Jim me and it was going to hurt.

126

Suddenly, the hall was full of screeches and laughter. Years of money and good food — these people knew how to behave. Dad — fuckin' Jim — was a prick because he was expected to be. It was the job. He was good at it; he excelled.

— What sort of a name is Victor?

— Dad —!

— I mean, where does it come from? What's the history?

— It's just a name, I said.

It was the best I could do. My notoriety, my adult credentials, were hiding behind the drum kit, shivering.

— Leave him alone, said Rachel.

She patted my arm and patted her father's arm. We headed for one of the rooms at the front of the house. She patted my arse. She didn't pat his. I was ahead.

Meat was carved and matching bowls of vegetables were passed around. Mum held on to my shoulder as she leaned in and lowered a strange jug of gravy, a thing like a potty, onto the table. There was a tit in my ear. I didn't look at Jim. He carved right through to the dish. I half expected Mum — her weight there on my shoulder — to keep going, to topple across me onto the table. But she didn't. She let go of me and sat, thank Christ, a few stops down the way.

— Yummy.

Someone said *Yummy*. My girlfriend said *Yummy*. Her siblings agreed, her father grunted. My mother cooked a decent Sunday dinner. There was a great consistency to everything she did. The chicken always tasted like her chicken. Given a pheasant, she'd have turned it into chicken. Sunday in our house was one smell, one taste, one quite happy memory. This, though, was wild and unrepeatable. There were things in this gravy. An onion — a whole onion — slid over the lip of the potty when I poured some of it onto my plate. I'd never had to pour my own gravy before. The onion — I didn't know what it was at first — fell onto the plate. I was sitting alone; there were empty chairs on either side of me. I looked across at Rachel. She grinned at me and chewed. She gave me a little wave with the hand that held her fork. But the gravy — it was black. It was alive. The onion was the blood-covered head of one of the unborn babies I'd been writing and talking about. I stuck some of the gravy to the side of a carrot — glazed — and managed to get it to my mouth without lowering my head too far. And, Jesus — the taste. This was the Southside. This was what it was all about. There was wine in there, and history. This stuff went back to the Norsemen. It went straight to the blood. I wanted to beat my chest.

   — Every — thing alright? Mum asked the table.

   — Fab.

   —Yumm-eee.

   — Do you have Sunday dinner at home — Vic —
She looked at me.

   — tor?

   — On Sundays, I said. — Yeah.

Dad stared at me, hard. He was going to Jim me till I bled. But I had the secret now: I was filling myself with his gravy. I'd Jim him right back.

— So, he said. — You're in favour of abortion and all that, are you?

— Dad —

— It's a question.

And fair enough, it *was* a question. But I had a whole onion in my mouth for the first time in my life. A dead baby's head, and I'd just bitten into it. It was full of boiling water that was now melting my gums and peeling the roof off my mouth.

—Yes, I said, but no one understood me.

I'd decided that I'd charge straight at Dad when he declared war. But my courage had gone unnoticed. My Yes sounded nothing like Yes. It sounded like a quick death.

— Are you alright, Victor?

— What's wrong with him?

I'd swallowed the onion — my decision. I couldn't bite into it again and I couldn't let it drop from my mouth back into the gravy. A scalding lump was moving down my throat. It was getting no less hot and I wasn't convinced it was moving at all. I picked up the glass of red that Dad had poured before we'd sat down, and knocked back most of it. It must have done something. The outer layers of the onion contracted, and I was able to swallow the thing. I could feel the wine rushing after it.

Rachel rubbed my back. I didn't know how she'd got there, from the far side of the table to right beside me.

— Okay?

I wasn't. I was far from okay. I'd never be okay. I wiped my eyes.

— Okay?

I could feel the onion, defeated but still evil, waiting to leap back out. Rachel's hand was gone. She patted my head and went back to Esther and Maeve at the other side of the table. I wiped my eyes. I could see better now.

— Is he alright?

— Is it something he does?

I smiled.

— Sorry about that, I said.

I'd forgotten about abortion. Everyone had. Except Dad. His frown couldn't mask his delight. His daughter had got herself stuck with an eejit, a Northside gutty who couldn't even eat.

— Tell us a bit about your book.

The attack didn't come from Jim this time. It came from Esther. In her bid to become Dad's little girl. I could feel the onion turning. Dad's little onion.

— Well — , I said.

— It's great, said Rachel.

She wasn't defending me; I knew that immediately. She'd looked through the stack of pages on the table in the flat. She'd found four pages, maybe five, that were coherent, or could have been called an extract. I knew I'd been caught and I couldn't feel grateful. She wasn't backing me up; she was hiding me. She was actually making me up. I couldn't be grateful, but I was. I smiled at Rachel. She smiled at me. Mum smiled. Maeve smiled.

Esther didn't smile.

— What's it about? she asked again.

— Well, I said. — Ireland.

— Oh, terrific, said Dad. — Another book about Ireland. Badly needed, I say.

— About what's wrong with Ireland, I said.

I could look straight at him, wait for the next attack. I'd be writing the book; it was in me.

— So, he said.

He pushed a chunk of beef into his mouth and chewed, and stared, and smiled, and swallowed.

— Tell us, he said. — What's wrong with Ireland?

— It's a book, Dad, said Rachel. — Not a list.

— I was talking to your boyfriend, said Jim.

He didn't look at her.

— I haven't had the benefit of being able to read the work in progress while sitting up in bed.

There was a gap then for a gasp. But no one gasped. Maeve nudged Rachel. It was the nicest thing I witnessed all day.

— What is wrong with Ireland? he asked. — Victor.

That was the problem. "I don't really know," should have been my answer. Or "I don't really know *yet*." The Church, politics, inequality, being stuck in the past, the political clout of the farmers. These were my targets but I hadn't been able to do much with them. I'd been felt up by a Christian Brother but I didn't blame the Church for that. I didn't know how to blame the Church; that came decades later. I knew the dominance of the Catholic Church was a bad thing but I didn't know how to expand on that, or even start. But: this is important: I was going to write the book: I was writing the book. I believed that. I knew it.

It was the word "boyfriend", the way her father had used it. The nudge, the push. It was a silly word, and childish. It was an order: ditch him. So I asked her, later.

— Will we get married?

She looked at me. She giggled — she *giggled*.

— Yes, she said. — We will.

Then she laughed like a woman.

— Why are we doing this? she asked.

And I told her the truth.

— Because I love you.

— And I love you, she said.

And that was true too.

She saved me. That was what Rachel did. She saved me and, later, she carried me. Her assertiveness, the way she grabbed me, pulled me into her, turned her back and remained the boss, her willingness to cry, the way she took sex, took and gave — I can see now that it saved me. It stunned me and made me. I'd fallen in love with an adult. I wasn't a fraud; I was a slow starter.

We moved into the loft soon after. It was right over Rachel's kitchen, in Temple Bar. Temple Bar then wasn't Temple Bar now. People puked and shouted, but far less of them. There was a local population, working-class people. There were a few good pubs, a couple of restaurants. There was the Project Arts Centre. There were artists and chancers. The cobblestones were genuine; they hadn't been left there for their charm. It was easy to feel special in Temple Bar. It was easy to think of Berlin or Prague.

132

Rachel unlocked the door. She pushed it open a few feet and we waited for the noises inside to stop. We said nothing. She pushed again but there was something inside, in the way. I leaned in, past her, and looked for the light switch. But it was bright enough already. We could see the line of windows, a whole wall of them. There were no blinds or curtains. It was late morning, about midday. I stepped in. I looked behind the door, to see what had been blocking it.

— Oh, God —

— What?

It was a dead pigeon. He was stiff but uneaten — a big grey lad.

— Is it a rat? she asked, although she was right behind me and the prospect wasn't slowing her down.

— No, I said.

The place was full of pigeons. Two of the windows were open and two more were missing their glass. There were white streaks of shit on the floorboards. We walked to the middle of the room. It was quite a stroll; the place seemed vast. There were no hiding places, just four empty corners and the windows. There was nothing indoors about the place. We might as well have been standing in the middle of a park. And we were living there a week later. There was no escape. I had to work.

And I did. Because she did. Rachel isn't a television invention. One thing you'll have noticed about Rachel if you've been following her career, if you've been watching her hair get slightly shorter by the year: she never says she works hard. She never boasts. She never spoofs. She claims nothing special, nothing God- or blood-given. She never claims an interesting history, or a struggle to get to the top. Those of you who watch carefully will know that quite often Rachel says nothing. Not because she's letting the men at it, but because she doesn't need to. They hate her, the men. They love her and hate her. Because they need her. They're expendable; Rachel isn't. The show will go on without them but there's no show without Rachel. The producers have tried to find her match. It's part of the show's appeal, why *Hit the Ground Running* comes back every autumn. Is there an entrepreneur out there who will knock Rachel Carey off her fuckin' perch? So far, no, there isn't.

I woke to Rachel clattering below me. I could measure her day while I lay on the mattress — we'd no bed for a while — in the centre of our huge room and heard the added voices and smelled the recipes climbing in through the gaps in the painted floorboards. There was Rachel and then there were other women — girls — down there. This is true: Rachel was the first person in Ireland to refer to her employees as "the team". Never "my team". And the team got bigger.

I worked too. I rolled over the clothes she always threw around and I went across to the table. I had a desk but it was daft, an old school desk with an inkwell. I could never sit back, I couldn't cross my legs. Out of place, it was almost sinister. Rachel had bought it in one of the antique shops on Francis Street. A present for me. I never used it — except for the photographs.

Because we fell for it. Rachel's work was real. So was mine, but she needed the publicity. The mothers of the party girls, and the women who worked for the men who decided that the product they were launching would sell more if the trays were being carried by pretty women with degrees, serving food that tasted great and looked un-Irish; they were Rachel's market. So the photos began to appear. Rachel with a tray; Rachel and two, three, four other women, all holding trays; Rachel stirring a cauldron; Rachel tasting her grub; Rachel behind the wheel of the van. *Look! A woman driving a van!* I stayed out of the way. I never went down to the kitchen. I could get in and out of the building without going in there. She did her work and I did mine. I wrote two chapters — I think I wrote two complete chapters. I can't remember the opening sentence. I can't remember a word. I typed the first chapter twice, word for word. I remember thinking it would give me the energy, work me up for the second chapter. And it did. I remember the blank page. I remember hammering out "Chapter Two", and I could keep going; there were words queuing up. I filled the page in a couple of minutes. Then I typed that page out again. I think I was writing about the 1916 Rising. I think I remember tapping out the date and liking its look on the page — and that got me on to the next page.

I'd get the bus or a taxi out to RTE every second or third Sunday and I'd say one controversial thing. On one occasion I said that Leaving Cert students should be issued with condoms when they were walking out of school on Friday afternoons. One of the panellists, an ageing member of Youth Defence, slapped me during the ads. She stood up from her place at the round table, came around and hit me hard. Her engagement ring cut my ear. She was back in her seat, shuffling her leaflets, when the studio light came back on. A researcher crept in and handed me her hankie.

That was the job. Now and again I said something shocking. I stirred it up. There was an honesty to it. I usually meant what I said. It made me hated, and never quite loved. It made me that prick. That twerp. That fuckin' maggot. *How did he end up with her?*

How did he end up with her? How did they know? It was Rachel's fault. I see that now. But it's meaningless, and stupid. It was no one's fault. I jumped at it. *That twerp fucks that girl.* I learnt the verb, "to fuck", from Rachel. Where I came from, where and when I grew up, men rode women. There were other words, and they stayed for a while, but riding was what it was. *I rode, you rode, he rode, we rode* and, sometime in the late 80s, *she rode.* No one fucked where I came from. Pregnancy was the result of sexual intercourse; everything else was riding. But Rachel didn't ride and she certainly wasn't ridden: Rachel fucked. I left my country and my class behind and started fucking Rachel. And I wanted the world to know that I was fucking Rachel.

There's a joke I heard years ago, about an Irishman who ends up on a desert island with Claudia Schiffer, after a plane crash. There's just the two of them, sitting on the sand. After a few days of this, she moves closer

136

to him. "Do you wish to ride me, Dermot?" she says. "Jesus, Claudia," he says. "Like — are you sure?" "Yes," she says. "We will be here for quite some time, I think. And the days are quite long — yes?" So, they start riding. All day. And Claudia falls hopelessly in love with him. This goes on for months until one day, the Irishman stands up and moves down the beach a bit and sits by himself. Claudia gets up and follows him. "Dermot?" she says. "Is something the matter?" "Ah, sure," he says. "I'm just a bit down in the dumps." "Is there something I can do to help?" she asks him. "Well," he says. "This might sound mad. But would you mind if I called you Des?" She looks at him, then says, "Alright. I will permit this." "Great," he says. "Brilliant, thanks." He's holding a piece of charcoal that he found on the beach. He shows it to Claudia and he says, "And, like — would you mind if I drew a moustache on you?" And she looks at him again, and says, "Alright, Dermot. This, too, I will permit." "Ah, great — thanks." He draws a rough moustache on her, then stands back. Then he grabs her shoulders, shakes her, and says, "Des! Des! You won't believe who I've been riding for the last three months!"

I knew how Dermot felt. But I didn't have to draw a moustache on Rachel. She drew one on me. Envy is a wild, reluctant form of respect. Men envied me, and women did too. And, for a while, they listened to me, not because I'd become one of the country's sharper, more incisive minds, but because I was riding Rachel Carey.

She started it. I never went down to her kitchen and the photographers never came up to our loft. And they only started coming up when we started calling it the loft. I don't remember what we called it before that. The flat? The room? I could phone Rachel now and ask her. She'd be friendly, nice; she'd ask me how I was. She'd laugh when I asked her about the loft. *Jesus, Victor — happy days.* I won't, though. I won't phone her. She'd ask me why I wanted to know. I can't think of a lie and I'm not going to tell her the truth. *I'm writing a book.* Her silence would destroy me, even the few seconds before she'd tell me she was delighted.

I could blame the phone. She needed to have a line extension upstairs; she didn't want the phone to go unanswered when the kitchen was empty. There was only one phone company in the country back then. They didn't have customers; they had beggars. Not even Rachel could warm them. But her father got someone he knew to sort it out for her. We had a phone beside the bed and I began to know Rachel at work. The phone would ring. She could be gasping, crying, biting my shoulder, then pick it up and sound like a sedated continuity announcer.

— Meals on Heels, Rachel speaking — hi.

It was fun, once she made it clear that I wasn't to distract her.

— When I'm on the phone, I'm not on you. Agreed?

I nodded. Agreed. Because I didn't believe her. She'd eventually agree to masturbate me while she explained the difference between samosas and poppadoms to some Monkstown mother who was trying to sort out a

Holy Communion. But she didn't. When Rachel was at work, I wasn't there. I listened to her explain that, as far as she knew, the Catholic Church had no objection to Indian food.

— You might try the Archbishop's Palace. Or I could, if you want. But there are nuns in India, aren't there? Mother Teresa — exactly. And priests — missionaries, yes. I'll check for you. No, it's no problem — it's as well to know, yes.

I knew not to laugh or try to let her see that I was listening.

— No, we don't strip, I heard her tell another customer.

There was no indignation in her voice, no pause; it was as if she was being asked about an ingredient.

— Nothing like that — no. We serve food.

I didn't have to ask her how work was going, because I knew. And she sometimes glanced at the pages I left on the desk. We both knew.

We knew nothing. I was always strategic about what I left on view. I had to be. She, on the other hand, was becoming a phenomenon and I was smug enough to think that it was all about cooking.

She announced — be fair: she asked. She asked if it would be okay if a photographer from *Irish Tatler* came up the stairs.

— *Irish Tatler?*

I pretended I'd never heard of it. I had, and I'd seen it. But I'd never looked inside it.

— Irish?

— Yes.

— Who reads that?

— Women in dentists' offices, husbands who have a quick flick through it while their wives are in the loo. Clients.

— Okay, I said. — What is a tattler, anyway?

— No idea.

— Where will I go?

— You can stay — it won't be a problem. In fact — listen — you could be working in the background.

And that was it. We'd been photographed together before, once, in the borrowed apartment in Dalkey. Kids in a posh adult world. This was different. We were at home. We were the adults. There I was, my back to the camera, wearing the shirt the photographer had told me to wear. There's one where I'm standing, leaning forward slightly, reading something on the desk, the window in front of me. I'm JFK, and Martin Sheen, in the White House. I can't remember what I was reading; it might have been something I'd written.

The photos were of Rachel. I was the white shirt to her left. But then there was the one that made us an item. I was standing again, gazing at the empty room across the street, trying to decide when it had last been occupied. The mid-60s, I thought, and a whole family had lived in there. There was no evidence of this, except the stains and shadows — where a bed might have been pushed against the wall, where a large pot had bubbled on a hob that wasn't there any more, a line of holes in the wall where the hooks that had held the spare clothes might have been. My father had grown up in a room like that — he'd told me once, and my mother

140

had told me later, after he'd died. I missed him. For the first time in years, I think. Maybe for the first time — I don't know. But I was missing him, and wondering how looking across the street at an empty room could make that happen, how it could make my stomach drop, when I felt Rachel behind me. She leaned against me. I stayed still. I said nothing. She said nothing. I didn't turn. That was the photograph.

The next time — I can't remember the magazine — I was facing the camera. The time after that, we were standing beside each other, leaning into each other, being the couple. Then I sat at the typewriter and Rachel read over my shoulder while I typed *All work and no play makes Jack a dull boy*, again and again, until the sun did what the photographer wanted it to do.

I went home to my mother's house for three days at Christmas, so I could go to the pub with the lads I'd gone to school with. I had to knock on doors because I had no phone numbers. Four or five hadn't emigrated; three were still living at home with their parents.

— You've done well for yourself.
— Fuckin' hell, what's her name again?
— Rachel, I told them.
— That's right, said Frankie Best.
He didn't look like a man who'd once had a trial at Everton. That had been seven years before. He already looked like an ex-footballer.
— Posh bird, he said.
He nodded and smiled.

— And on the radio as well, said Kenny Peters. — Yeh fucker, yeh.

He was smiling too. I was still one of them — just about. I was riding her, so we were all riding her. I was doing it, going out there, getting myself known, riding beautiful women.

— Fair play, said Kenny. — But come here — don't start going on about abortion in here, d'you hear me? It's fuckin' Christmas.

— What's she do again?

— Does she take it up the gicker?

— Come here, but — d'you get paid for being on the radio? You don't, do yeh?

— I do, yeah.

— For fuck sake. You're paying for the next round, so. You still playin' the football?

— Not really.

They'd already forgotten that I never really played.

— He's too fuckin' busy. And you didn't tell us yet.

— What?

— If she takes it up the gicker.

They didn't expect an answer. They didn't want an answer. An answer would have appalled them. They respected their women and Rachel was one of theirs now, for the evening at least, or till I went out to the toilet. It was good to be there, in a packed pub full of people I used to know, men and women — mothers and fathers — who'd known me when I was a kid, who'd known my father, who liked my mother. And their sons and daughters — boys I'd grown up running away from; and other boys, men now too, who'd been a bit careful, a bit frightened, a bit clever like me. And the girls I'd grown up staring at, some of them already looking worn and defeated, and sexy; others still getting the hang of not being children. I don't remember seeing Fitzpatrick's sister — or Fitzpatrick — that night; I don't remember looking for her. It was good to be there. Even though I was never going to pick up my pint and wander, slap the backs, shake the hands, kiss cheeks, grab arses. But I was there and I liked it and I felt almost at home.

And I *was* at home. I think I was. With the lads I'd grown up with, who'd been in on the terror and crack of the Christian Brothers, who'd stared at German porn mags with me, who'd got drunk with me the first time. I don't think I'm being sentimental and I don't think I was then. (I was twenty-three, I think.) Fucking Rachel was one thing. Being the man who was riding Rachel was another. It was why I was there. Not to gloat, although yes. But it explained me. It made sense of me and my desertion. It allowed them to forgive me. And me — it allowed me to forgive myself. They could bring me back in, bring me up to date.

— Moonshine's living over in Luton now, Frankie told me.

— I know, yeah. My mother told me.

— Married to an English bird, he is.

— What's she like?

— Don't know. He doesn't get his picture in the fuckin' papers all that often, you know.

There was no malice. This was slagging — it was love.

— Will we all go over?

It was my idea.

— To England?

— Yeah.

— What? Now?

— No.

— It's fuckin' Christmas.

— No. The new year. We can go to a match as well.

— Not fuckin' Luton.

— No — we can go on into London.

— Not fuckin' Spurs.

— Not fuckin' Arsenal.

— Will we do it, though? I asked them.

— Ah, yeah.

— January.

— Make it February — get a few quid together. March.

— Okay.

We drank to it. We laughed.

It was the last time I slept in my mother's house and it was the last time I went for pints with the lads. Two of them are dead. I miss them like I miss my father; I wish I'd known them.

CHAPTER
ELEVEN

I sat at the bar. If Fitzpatrick arrived, he'd drag in others; there'd be safety in numbers. He didn't turn up. I chatted with a man called Gerry and left after the second pint.

I'd gone to the edge of the estate. I'd walked there one Saturday morning, along the coast. I'd stopped at the corner where the road in joined the main coast road. I'd stood there and looked at the first couple of houses. They were still the same, but very different. So many cars, so few kids. No noise, except for traffic behind me on the main road. A woman came out of Kenny Peters's house. She was black. She shouted back through the front door — I don't think it was English she was roaring — and a pile of boys in jerseys came bailing out, trying to trip one another up with their hurleys. She filled the car, and they were gone. Down, I guessed, to the GAA club. I didn't move further in. The disappointment, the guilt. The guilt. I stood a while longer. I'd set out quite early, before eight o'clock. The heat was beginning to press down on me. I'd have loved a Coke or a Fanta. I hadn't tasted Fanta in years. I knew where the shop was. I knew it would still be there, with a different name — Mace, Spar, or Costcutters. It had been the Mint when I'd left. It was just a bit further down the road. But I didn't move. I didn't feel entitled to. I hoped a car might approach, a half-familiar face under the creases and fat might stare out and the car might slow down and stop after it had passed me. *Is that you?* I had it planned out, written. I'd turn. *Yeah — is that* you? Frankie or Will. Or maybe a woman. Fitzpatrick's sister. It didn't happen.

I was used to being alone. I don't think I felt lonely. I missed being married but I'm not sure that I missed Rachel. The aloneness was cleaner now. I wasn't surrounded by her world. I didn't have to hide.

I didn't like Fitzpatrick. But he brought me so far back; that was the appeal — the lure. It wasn't nostalgia. I don't think it was. I was never going to knock on the front door of my old house and ask to see my bedroom. I missed my mother, and I admit that I started missing her after Rachel asked me to leave. But I was never going to knock on old doors.

I wondered why I wasn't like him — or, if I could have been like him. How would I have been, *who* would I have been, if I'd stayed? I wanted to thump my stomach, accept my age. I wanted to stare at women and not care that they saw me. I wanted some of his disaster. His sister intrigued me too. I wanted to face what might have been. I wanted to see the wreckage and like it.

I sat at the bar again. The man I'd chatted with the night before, Gerry; he'd told me about his days since he'd taken early retirement. He walked a lot; he volunteered. He was a bore, but I'd liked him. And I'd

146

liked the feeling, accepting that I liked him. It had been a long time since I'd let that happen. Gerry wasn't there this time. He'd said something about walking with some other people — a walking club — in Wicklow. Lough Dan, he'd said. I'd thought I'd ask him about the club when I saw him again.

— For fuck sake — the man.

It was Fitzpatrick. He dropped his arm across my shoulders. Still in the pink shirt and shorts. Huge and clammy.

— The man they couldn't hang.

He let go of me.

— Will you have a pint? I asked.

— Does the Pope shit in the fuckin' woods? he said. — I'll have a rake of pints but one'll do for starters.

He looked around to see who was appreciating him. I wanted to get out; he was too near, too there. But he had me cornered. Getting away would have involved getting around him. He'd have stopped me. He'd have picked me up and thrown me back up on my stool. He'd have laughed and snarled. I had to accept it: I was exactly where I wanted to be.

I ordered a pint of Heineken for him.

— Are you not having one?

— I'm grand.

— Grand my hole, he said. — Have a fuckin' pint. I'm not drinking alone.

— I have one.

— It's nearly gone. Here, Carlo. Stick on a pint for this poor miserable fucker.

He clapped his hands.

— Well.

He wiped the back of his neck with a hand and rubbed the hand on the side of his shorts.

— First man to mention the weather gets a dig in the snot, he said.

That got a laugh. I'd gone from being alone in a quiet pub to being one of the lads in a busy one. But Fitzpatrick still had me cornered. He stood between me and the loose group of other men. I could only get into the gang if he let me in.

— I saw your ex there, Pat, said one. — I thought she was looking well.

— Where did you see her?

— In the scratcher beside me.

— Fuck off now.

I was allowed to laugh. But I had to look around Fitzpatrick to see who was talking. I shifted my stool a bit, dragged it away from the counter without standing up. But it didn't work. I was still stuck behind him. They were talking about a woman now, someone they'd known all their lives.

— She was always a slapper, that one.

— I saw her in SuperValu. My Jesus — you'd swear she was on her way to a fuckin' disco.

Who? I wanted to shout. *Who?*

— Ah, now, she makes the effort.

— And I'll tell you now. I would.

— So would I — no fuckin' qualms.

Who?

— Talking about qualms, said Fitzpatrick. — D'you want to guess who this guy's married to?

He stood aside. He was unveiling me and he'd caught me off guard, my pint at my mouth. There were four men looking at me. Fitzpatrick put a big, wet open hand on the back of my head and pushed me forward.

— Yis'll never guess, he said.

They looked at me.

A mouth opened.

— Who?

I'd have to speak. One of Fitzpatrick's fingers was tapping the back of my head. I admit it: I wanted to name her.

— Rachel Carey, I said.

— Who?

— Off the telly, said Fitzpatrick.

— Who?

They were delighted, although they didn't know who she was yet. She could have read the news, done the weather, delivered the gossip, cooked, sung, renovated, lost weight, hugged troubled teenagers, spoken Irish, any of the stuff they never watched but knew about.

— Which one is she?

The question wasn't directed at me. I'd given them the name but they might as well have seen it on a screen. I wasn't there. The four of them were throwing Rachel around, like dogs with a toy. It struck me: Fitzpatrick wasn't one of them either. He was outside, like me, looking in.

— *Hit the Ground Running*, he said.

— What?

He was interrupting them.

— She's your woman on *Hit the Ground Running*.

— Which one is that?

Fitzpatrick was bang against me. He had me pinned to the counter, but he was fading. They were messing, pretending — calm. They were acting the eejit. They were the lads I'd grown up with. They'd turn to me in a while.

— She crosses her legs when she's bored, said Fitzpatrick.

That stunned me. He was right: she did. And they knew what he meant and who she was. Rachel's legs were famous.

— Her?

— Fuckin' hell.

They knew who she was. That part was over. They looked at me now. Not with new respect, or any respect. She was off the telly, so I was off the telly. She was a celebrity, and that made me an alien. These men were tight; they'd been growing up and old together. Fitzpatrick wasn't one of them — I didn't think he was now — but they knew him to see. They tolerated him. A bit of banter, a comment on the weather, the football, Cheryl Cole or the cunts in government, five of their minutes once or twice a week; that was Fitzpatrick's lot. But he knew me and that made him useful. It made me human.

— This prick went to school with me, he told them now.

— Is that right? said one of them. — What school was that?

— St Martin's CBS.

— Oh, for fuck sake.

— Fuck off now, said Fitzpatrick. — It wasn't the worst.

— Oh, yes, it was, I said.

Research. The word bumped about in my head, back where Fitzpatrick had been tapping my skull. *I'm going to write about this. I'm going to write — I'm going to keep writing.*

They laughed.

— Have you met your man who presents it? one of them asked me.

Hit the Ground Running was a mix of *The Apprentice* and *Dragons' Den*, an endurance test for young entrepreneurs "of all ages". The presenter was Will O'Gorman, the former rugby player. The show had been running for five years and O'Gorman and Rachel had both joined "Team HGR" at the start of the second season. It had quickly become the Will and Rachel show.

— I have, yeah, I said.

— What's he like?

— Grand.

— Is he not up his own arse?

— Not really, I said. — He's sound.

I was giving them the answer they wanted. O'Gorman was actually a cunt. Not that I'd met him. Rachel had told me, the last time we'd sat in the kitchen together.

— I hate saying it, Victor, I hate the word. But he's a cunt — he really is.

I thought at the time that she was talking about me, and I was right. I thought too that hearing her call him a cunt confirmed my suspicions that they were having some kind of affair, but I was probably wrong. The lads here needed to know that Will O'Gorman, or "WOG", as he was known among the guys who knew their rugby, was one of them. I could see it in front of me. I knew Will, so they knew Will. Fitzpatrick was still there, still hanging over me, but he wasn't one of us.

They were waiting for more.

— He gives the impression of being a bit lackadaisical, I said. — But, actually, he's — he's very professional.

They nodded; they'd known it all along.

— So Rachel says, I told them. — And he's a bit mad too.

They loved that.

— Pints? one of them asked.

He was talking to the other three.

— Stupid question.

— G'wan.

He looked at me.

— Yourself?

— Thanks, I said.

He didn't want to look at Fitzpatrick. I could see that. They all wanted Fitzpatrick to go away. But he'd brought a gift, so they couldn't be rude. I watched the man who was buying the round trying to think of Fitzpatrick's name.

— No point in asking you, he said. — You'd never say no to a pint. What's that piss you're on?

— Heineken, said Fitzpatrick. — The official beer of fuckin' rugby.

— The official beer of fuckin' nothing.

Fitzpatrick could feel himself being pushed from the shore.

— Would you trust him, though? he asked me.

He'd stepped away so he could look at me and get in among the other men.

— Who?

— WOG, he said. — He'd get up on anything, that fella.

— Ah now, said one of them. — None of that. Keep it clean.

They didn't like it.

— I trust my wife, I said.

I was smiling.

— With that fella around? said Fitzpatrick.

— You heard the man. Give it up.

— He's not even with her any more, said Fitzpatrick. — That's why he's here.

— Shut it, said the man who was buying the round. — We all have our issues, so fuck it. Enough.

I'd got rid of Fitzpatrick. He was still there but I could feel him floating away.

I'd seen these men before; I'd watched them. They flirted with women their own age, they gave the lounge girls plenty of space when they were passing through with the trays. They came in every second night, usually when I was leaving. I'd change that. I wanted this thing I'd missed out on, even a late glimpse of it.

— Though it has to be said, said one of the men. — She is a good-looking woman. No offence.

I smiled.

— God, yeah.

I kept smiling. I felt wretched. But the life I hadn't had, I was getting a bit of it now. The companionship, the ease of it, the acceptance — I was going to live it.

— We'll leave it at that, said the round-buyer. — We're fans.

— We fuckin' are.

We laughed.

I sat at the table, and wrote. *She pulled me to the floor by the sleeve of my jumper. Then she kneeled in front of me — she wasn't smiling. She turned her back and dropped onto her elbows.* I put on a record. I was listening to music again. I'd brought my record player and some of the records across from the house. I'd texted Rachel and asked her if I could take it. *Yes. X.* It had been in the hall when I rang the bell, the deck, speakers, amp, the wires all neatly coiled and in a Lidl bag. The cleaner, a Russian or Latvian woman — I could never remember her name — helped me get the speakers into the back of the car.

— Rachel isn't in, no?

— No.

— Okay.

I'd put the deck on the table, in front of me, behind the laptop. I'd get something better, a proper cabinet or something, but I quite liked the idea of looking up from the screen and seeing the record turning. I could hear myself in a studio, telling some big-eyed presenter about my work routine. *Vinyl? God, yeah. Right in front of me.* I played the first side of *Blood on the*

Tracks and wrote a page. I lifted the needle and left. I was happy, somehow; there was bounce in me. I was a man on his way to meet his friends.

I was worried about Fitzpatrick. I'd get the timing or the day wrong; there'd be no one there, or I'd be too early and be stuck with him. They'd never see me alone. I was thinking the way I'd done when I was a teenager. I'd stand at the front door and try to see through the pebbled glass, make sure it was Moonshine passing on the road outside and not Cyril Toner or some other spa, before I opened the door and got stuck. There was always the timing, always the gamble.

They were there, the men, whoever they were. I couldn't recall the last time I'd had to remember names, or the last time I'd thought it mattered. I didn't go straight across to them; I couldn't do that. I went to the bar, a bit to their left, and ordered my pint.

— Pint, please, Carl; thanks.

I looked around — no sign of Fitzpatrick. One of the men was looking my way. I gave him the chin lift, hello. He nodded, grimaced. One of his friends turned on his stool and looked.

— Ah — good man.

I was in.

— Are you alright for drink? I asked.

He looked at his own pint.

— I think we're alright, he said. — No — fuck it, go on ahead.

— Three pints, is it?

— Just three.

— No one in the jacks or gone for a smoke?

155

— No, he said. — It's just us tonight.

— Three more pints as well, Carl; thanks.

The man on the stool pushed it back and I became the fourth corner. Liam, Pat, Harry. They were the men there that night.

— I'm Victor, by the way.

— I googled yeh.

— And?

— Fuck all.

We laughed.

— Rachel always keeps her private life private, I said. — We were a bit stupid about that when we were younger.

— Wise move, said Liam.

— We were just talking about the football, said Pat. — The money — the amount the fuckers get paid.

— It's mad money, said Harry. — But it's there. The money's in football. So fair play to them.

— Your man that owns Liverpool, did you ever see his wife?

— Don't think so, said Harry.

— My Christ, said Pat. — Beautiful — fuckin' beautiful. Mature woman, you know. Beautiful.

— What's your point?

— No point. But it's all football. Today's game. The women and the money. Isn't it?

He looked at me. I smiled. I could tell: Pat was the fucker and he wanted to mention Rachel. *The women and the money.* But he left me alone. I paid for the pints and handed them around. They felt cold and great in my hand. I'd be drinking four pints before closing time. I was in the round. I was delighted — I really was. My gut, my body, felt open, ready to take its share.

The last time I'd paid attention to football I'd followed Derby County. I knew enough; announcing this would make me a serious football man. It would give me the needed decades and misery. But I knew nothing about Derby these days — who managed them, what Irish players played for them, the chances of promotion next season, the more recent history. I'd do my homework; I'd enjoy it. I'd fall back in love with Derby County.

I liked Harry. There was a bit of colour about him. The women liked Harry. I knew that before I saw the proof. Pat was a fat imp. A messer. He had edge and he was clever. He could read faces. He'd always known his place in the gang. I was a kid again, reading the signs. That was what had happened when my father died: I'd stopped being able to read.

— Here we go, said Pat.

My back was to the door but I knew: women had walked in. Pat was trying to make himself taller. Liam put his pint on the counter, grabbed his belt at the back and hoisted his jeans. Harry did nothing but the bit of tiredness in his face was gone. I knew what all of this meant: nothing. I'd turn and see a group of mature women — I love the word "mature". I could hear them, deciding what they'd have. I loved that about women — all those lived years and they still didn't know what they'd have to drink when they walked into a pub. Or they pretended not to know, and I loved the effort that went into it. They wouldn't be going wild, these women. They'd just add screams to the laughter coming up to closing time and they'd flirt — slightly — with my new friends, on the way back from the toilet or a smoke in the beer garden. They'd have known one another for years — school, weddings, house sales, breakups. They'd know the wives, ex-wives, husbands, ex-husbands.

Girls walk into a room. The boys sit up. Women in their late forties walk into a room. Men in their fifties sit up, straighten their backs, pull down the fronts of their hoodies. It made me want to cry. I felt I was going right back into the life I'd missed.

I still hadn't looked. The women had gone to one of the high tables near the row of windows. I heard the scrape of stools and I saw one of the lounge girls fill a tray with drinks and mixers and head over to them. Things settled. Liam's pint was back in his paw — he was a big man. Harry was waiting for Carl to see him, so he could show him four fingers and order his round.

— Where were we? said Liam.

— Right fuckin' here, said Pat.

— Going anywhere this year, Victor? Liam asked.

He'd used my name but it still took me a while to realise that he was talking to me.

— I doubt it, I said. — I've only moved in.

— Too much on.

— Yeah.

— Too fuckin' skint.

— That too. What about yourself?

158

What about yourself? I was doing well, I thought. I'd heard men say that, the uncles and my father, gathered in the hall and kitchen at home, when I was a child. *What about yourself? Ah sure* — I was back home, back across the river. There was definitely a novel in me.

— The Algarve, said Liam.

— You should see his place, said Pat. — Fuckin' magnificent.

There was something vicious in the words, envy sharpened to a point.

— You have a place there? I asked Liam.

— Kind of, he said.

— You should see it.

— A timeshare thing, said Liam.

— Great.

— Unbelievable, said Pat. — Two golf courses, by the way. Fuckin' two.

— Great.

— D'you play, yourself, Victor?

— No.

— Do you not?

— No, I said. — I never got round to it.

— Never too late, said Harry.

— I only started a few years back, said Pat.

— And you're still shite, said Liam.

— Fuck off, you.

Pat turned his eyes on me again.

— D'you have a place? Abroad, like?

— No, I lied.

It wasn't a lie, but it would have been a year before.

I saw the man I'd spoken to a few days back, Gerry, the hill walker. I nodded, smiled. He smiled back, and got back talking to his friend beside him. He was keeping an eye on the women too, I saw.

— We don't take it too seriously, said Harry.

— What?

— The golf.

— To avoid the disappointment, said Liam. — The same with everything. That's what it's all about now, isn't it? From here on in. Avoiding disappointment.

— Will you listen to fuckin' Aristotle.

Would I play golf? Would I go that far? I didn't think so. Catching up on Derby County would be enough, and probably a basic knowledge of current rugby. I'd have to get Sky Sports. I'd have to watch it.

These men had done alright. They'd coped with the mortgages, their kids were done or nearly done with school, their houses were a bit bigger than the ones they'd grown up in. Or, the houses they'd lived in before the break-ups. I knew nothing yet, but I was guessing that Harry was still married and sliding his arm around a wife and Pat was on his own in half a house or an apartment. I wasn't sure about Liam. I wasn't sure about anything. There was something about Pat's anger; he was still catching up, still grieving. Why did I care? I wanted to know them.

I couldn't go after my old friends. There'd been deaths, and I'd heard about a son's suicide, from my mother — I hadn't gone with her to the funeral. There'd been depression, alcoholism. There'd been bailiffs. There'd been successes too — there was a daughter lecturing in Harvard or Princeton. There'd been a Lotto win. There'd been divorces, a car crash, cancer, Parkinson's, strokes. The stories had dried up after my mother died. My old friends were more interesting than my new ones, I suspected. I was proud of them but I couldn't walk back in there. I spoke in the church at my mother's funeral. I didn't invite them back to the house or on to a hotel lounge or the local for soup and a pint. I went straight home after the graveyard. I kissed my sister goodbye and left. Rachel said nothing all the way home, back across to our side. My son wasn't there.

This was the fresh start. I thought. I hoped. Although Fitzpatrick was lurking somewhere. He'd know — he knew — more than I'd want known. He'd know facts and lies. But he wasn't there now. I suspected Fitzpatrick disappeared for spells.

I was starting my third pint. The place had filled up after ten o'clock. There were more people now trying to get to the bar. We were in the way, but the little upheavals were good-natured. I'd made room for a man, and I found myself looking over Pat's shoulder at the women while we talked about Rory McIlroy, *Fifty Shades of Grey*, and Brian O'Driscoll's retirement.

— D'you know him?

Pat had caught me on the hop. I was still looking over his head.

— Sorry — me?

— Who else? We don't know him.

— I met his father once, said Harry. — Nice man. Sold him a policy.

— D'you know him? Pat asked me again.

— Who?

— Too busy gawking at the women, said Pat. — BOD.

I thought he was talking about one of the women.

— O'Driscoll, he said.

— Oh, I said, and laughed. — No, I don't know him. Then I added a bit.

— Not really.

— You've met him.

— Yeah, I lied. — Shook his hand once or twice. Said Hello and Up the Northside.

They grinned.

— What about his wife? said Liam. — Amy.

— She was with him, I said. — It was a do — a charity thing.

My mother had loved that word, "do". Any event that involved putting on the good clothes had been a do. Rachel loved the word too. She'd be telling me where she was going — I'd be watching her at the dressing-table mirror. She never sat at it, although there was a stool. She leaned forward and down, into it. In our last years, she'd let her reading glasses slip from her head to her nose, and examine her work. It might be a twenty-first or a launch or, later on, when she really took off, supper with people from London. Whether the Queen was going to be there or a bunch of blonde kids making themselves vomit the birthday cake in the toilets, she'd hesitate, smile, and call it a do. She'd got the word from my mother. She'd loved my mother.

— Is she as good-looking in the flesh?

— Amy?

— Yeah.

— I didn't see that much of the flesh, I said. — Unfortunately.

I was one of them.

— Her shoulders were impressive, I told them. — Although not as impressive as his.

They laughed, and then I gave them what we needed.

— She's gorgeous, I said.

— Is she a friend of your wife's — or —?

— No, I said. — I don't think they'd know one another that well. There's the age difference.

— 'Course. I thought maybe — there aren't all that many celebrities in this country. Real ones, anyway, the genuine article. So I thought they'd bump into each other.

— There's a thought, said Harry.

— Rachel — , I said. — She actually lives very quietly.

— Especially since she threw you out.

That was the door opening wide. They were going to love slagging me. I was going to love being slagged.

One of the women came over.

— How're all the lads?

— How's it going, Brenda? said Pat.

— Ah, sure — fabulously.

— Any news of China?

— Well, there you go. She's in fuckin' China!

China was Brenda's daughter and she was in Beijing.

— Brilliant, said Liam.

She showed us a photo on her phone. The daughter on the Great Wall, holding up a banner — *The Great Wall of Me!* The mother was having a ball. She leaned on Pat's knees — he was up on a stool — while she searched for another photo. Pat opened his legs, so she'd slip between them.

— Stop that, you messer.

She slapped his thigh. They laughed. Pat and Liam looked like men who couldn't wait to see more photographs. Harry stood back a bit — a small bit. He was smiling but he wasn't looking as Brenda flicked through the snaps. I joined him.

— D'you have kids, yourself, Victor? he asked.

— I've a son, I said.

— What's he up to?

— He's away, I said.

That seemed to be enough. You reached an age when everyone's kids were away, or back. It wasn't just the economy. It had always been like that. In my world. In the world I thought I'd probably left.

— And you? I asked.

— I've four, he said. — One's away.

— The eldest?

— Yeah.

I knew enough. It was honest. I'd never have to remember their ages, genders, the points they'd got in the Leaving Cert, the college options, the little disasters. He'd never have to know that I hadn't seen my son in three years. That I had no photographs of him. That I didn't want to ask Rachel for one, because

164

then she'd know I didn't have any. She already knew. But I didn't want to hear or see her knowing.

— I used to have a place, I told Harry — just Harry.

The other two were still glued to Brenda. She'd stay another minute, then she'd smile at Harry and look at me before she went back to her friends.

We'd had a pied-à-terre in Paris. Rachel still had it. I'd never see it again. In fact, I'd only been in it once. I'd loved that term, pied-à-terre, and the silliness of it. Millionaires paying — borrowing — fortunes for their little foot on the ground. It always came with "It's only". *It's only a pied-à-terre.* I'd loved listening to Rachel apologising for owning an apartment in the world's best city. We'd had a place in Barcelona for a while before that. Five years. We stayed in it twice. It had been in both our names, although Rachel had paid for it. I'd hinted that I might go there to work, to get away from the distractions. Once upon a time, ten, even five years earlier, she'd have said it was a great idea. She'd have smiled her delight. She'd have said that she'd come down to me at the weekends. We'd have embraced, she'd have felt my erection, and looked straight back at me. This time, though, she sold it.

— We had a place in Paris, I told Harry.

— Nice.

— Yeah, I said. — Beautiful. Great part of the city. Near Saint Germain des Prés.

— Ah, yeah, he said. — It's lovely there.

— Isn't it? I said. — It's not mine now. Unfortunately.

— Does she —?

— Ah, yeah. Yeah, she still has it. I didn't fight.

— Can't be easy.

— It's hell, I said. — *Was* hell.

I shrugged. Enough said. I wouldn't bore him and I wouldn't make him squirm. Brenda was going. She shoved her iPhone down into the back pocket of her skinny jeans. She smiled at Harry. And she looked at me, and smiled. I smiled back. She'd know soon who my wife was. She might have known already. That was probably good. I didn't know.

— D'you remember her when she was in school? said Liam.

I could tell it wasn't a new question; this was a routine. I might have seen Brenda, myself, when she was in school. The house I'd grown up in was only three miles away.

— She'd have put the horn on a corpse. Back in the day.

— The daughter's a ringer, isn't she?

— Unbelievable — so fuckin' alike. It's funny.

— It is.

The chat rolled on, away from Brenda, back to holidays and work and decking and a funeral that would be coming up — someone's mother was on the way out. We talked about the fashion for bringing the dead back to their houses for the last night before the burial.

— It's the old way.

—Yeah, but it stopped being the way years ago. And now it's suddenly the way again. Except someone in the house always fuckin' explains that it's the old way. If it

166

was really the old way, you wouldn't need someone to explain it every time. Would you — am I right?

— Yeah.

— And no. You're not right.

— I have to be, said Liam. — It never happened until a few years ago. There was the removal to the church. So you got the whole thing out of the way on your way home from work. Drop in to the church, say I'm sorry for your troubles. Make sure you're seen. Do the decent thing. Then go home. That was the way it was for all of our lives.

— Because we grew up here. In Dublin, said Pat.

— What's that got to do with it?

— That's how it was done in Dublin.

— Yeah — and? Your fuckin' point, please.

— It was always different in the country, said Pat.

— Yeah, said Harry. — I've been to a lot of wakes. In houses. Down where my dad comes from.

— So what? Why has this culchie practice suddenly come to Dublin? Why do we need to pretend that we live in fuckin' farmhouses in the 1920s?

— My wife, I said.

That grabbed them.

— She had a catering business, I said. — For years.

— Meals on Tits.

— Heels.

— That's right.

They laughed, stunned. Like kids who'd expected to be battered by the teacher but had got away with it.

— Anyway, I said. — She started catering for funerals. For wakes.

167

— Southside wakes.

— Yeah. Coddle and griddle cake, and bacon and cabbage.

— That's gas.

— So it's true, I said. — The wake came back into fashion.

— You can't beat a good coddle, by the way.

— Has to be good, though. There's nothing worse than a bad one.

— Like eating your dinner straight out of a brown wheelie.

— And tell us, said Pat. — Did they dress up in their bunny outfits?

— Who?

— The girls. Serving the food.

— They didn't wear bunny outfits, I told him.

— Did they not?

— No. Never.

— I thought I remembered photographs. Back in the day.

— No.

— Grand.

— Your parents still with us, Victor? Harry asked.

— No.

— It's your favourite fuckin' word, that, said Pat.

He was a fucker but I was starting to really like him.

— Well, they're dead, I said. — In fairness.

— And you'd never lie, of course.

— No — of course not. Never.

We left together. They seemed to know when it was time to go. We'd had four pints. Maybe that was it —

they all bought a round, then went. Four was enough. You could feel a bit pissed. You'd had a bit of a night but you'd feel okay in the morning. Carl and the younger barman — the men called him One Direction — were still serving but no one suggested that we have another. Like the geese migrating, they just knew — it was time to go home.

We walked past the line of taxis, past the line of houses that looked like they'd never been lived in. Five of them in a tight row, bang up against the pub car park; there were identical rusting padlocks on four of the gates. The identical front hedges hadn't been cut in a long time, if ever. We went straight past them; I didn't ask for a history. I'd pick it up — who had owned the land, who he'd sold it to, the good timing, the bad timing, the killing, the fall. The next corner was mine but they were crossing the street, on to the next corner or the next. I'd find out. I'd get to know where they lived and where they used to live — addresses, names, neighbours, fights. I'd absorb all the details and contribute some of my own.

They knew I'd be turning.

— What are they like inside?

They knew I was in one of the apartments.

— Fine, I said. — Grand.

— It's a nondescript oul' building.

— Yeah, but it's okay, I said. — It'll do. I like it.

I'd expected — I'd hoped for another slagging. I hoped they'd see that I was walking home into something wild. I was their man on the dark side. I'd tell them about fat men on the stairs and the sound of smashing glasses. I'd give it to them, dish it out once or twice a week. I'd share the banging and the moving beds. I'd make it up. I'd have to. I'd sat there, I'd lain there, waiting for the creaks and groans, heels and whimpering, the gunfire. But very little — nothing. I'd forgotten I'd thought I was renting a flat in a brothel, until now. I'd tell them about the feral cats. And the foxes I'd seen gliding across the car park.

— See you, lads, I said.
— Yeah — see yeh.
— 'Night.
— Good luck.

I didn't say I'd see them again. I didn't ask when they'd be there again. I knew they'd be talking quietly about Rachel and bunny outfits and wondering what she'd ever seen in me.

I went across the car park, went a bit quicker. I charged up the stairs; I was dying for a piss. The phrase, "dying for a piss", was there — dying, dying. I got the key in the lock, got to the toilet and had a piss that seemed to go on for minutes — I might have fallen asleep for a while, standing up. I sat at the table and thought about writing, and forgot. But I would. I knew I'd write. I was in a new life — my head was in the hedge and I was battling through it. Nearly there — I could see it. I thought about toast. Making some. Eating it. I didn't have any bread. I got up and checked. I'd no bread. I'd write about that. Checking the bread for mould while the woman above me told the fat man from the Midlands to fuck her, in Czech. Or something. *Your farm has very many hectares?* He'd have been to a wake that night. That was what had brought him up to Dublin. Something like that. I went back to the table. I didn't want to write on the pages already on the table. They were for something else — the novel. I wanted to keep them clean for that. My bag was leaning against one of the table legs. I found the Moleskine notebook Rachel had given me years before — years before she'd copped on that I wouldn't be putting anything in the notebooks she kept giving me. *31/7/14. Girl — fat farmer — Czech. Or Polish. Wake. Sadness. Brother/old girlfriend?* I'd take it from there. It would become something. A short story. I could feel it in me, written. Just waiting. I was ready for another piss, then bed. I'd text Rachel. *Using the notebook — writing a short story and a novel. X.* No, I wouldn't do that. I left the phone on the table, to make sure I didn't do something stupid. I went into the toilet. I came out. I emptied my pockets. I'd lost my phone. I remembered — it was on the table. I remembered why. I sat on the bed. Derby County. I needed to remember about that too. Getting myself up to date. Would he know how many acres made a hectare? Would they get into that — the metric system? It would become the rhythm of their riding — her backing into him, trying to get him done and out, then becoming involved — she'd be a country girl herself. A peasant. She'd know exactly how many acres there were in a hectare, or the other way round. I needed the notebook. I got up. I fell back. I laughed — I think. I got up. I took the notebook from the table, and the pen, and the phone.

CHAPTER
TWELVE

— How's the lovely Rachel? Síle Ní Bhuachalla asked me.

We were on air. The country knew who she was referring to.

— She's well, thanks.

— Great. Still planning the family?

— Spectacularly, I answered.

Rachel had said in some Sunday interview that we — *we* — were planning on having children. *At some point in the future — loads of them, actually. But not just now.* That meant one thing. Contraception. Rachel visited the Irish Family Planning Association clinic on Cathal Brugha Street. She walked past the prayer groups reciting the rosary outside. And she was recognised. *Hoor. Slut. Prostitute.* She was followed. She felt the drops of holy water hit the back of her head. She saw the spit on the back of her jacket when she got home to the loft. And she gagged. But she let the jacket drop to the floor and decided to deal with it later.

I went with her to Cathal Brugha Street. I spoke about it and I wrote about it. For months. Rachel was being honest. She wanted sex but she didn't want a baby. She wanted the babies but not until she wanted them. She'd said it out loud. And she was reviled and loved — adored, admired. People liked her and were wary, frightened of. her. She was sent razor blades in envelopes, and holy medals. And recipes and job requests. And proposals and shit and threats and invitations. And orders. Business boomed.

She came home one night from a visit to her parents and sat on the side of the bed and cried. I went towards her but she stiffened.

— Don't — please —

I sat at the end of the bed and watched her.

— Tea?

She shook her head three or four seconds after I'd asked the question. I felt it in me — I was the boy at the end of the bed. Sitting, waiting, for hours, for my mother to sit up and stop whimpering. It was the way I'd found her day after day when I came home from school in the months after my father died. I stood up now and went across to the table. I sat down and I wrote. I really did write that night, about the rot that was at the heart of Ireland. Until I felt Rachel standing behind me. I remembered my mother's face when she sat up, trying to make herself the way she should have been — not the woman who'd been lying in the bed. There were minutes sometimes when there was a fight between the two women. Eventually — always — my mother won. She was grieving, but I didn't understand that. I didn't grieve. I never expected my father to come back. I just didn't feel that he was gone. He was my father, there or not there. It didn't matter. My mother would smile after she sat up.

— God — the state of me. I must've fallen asleep. Put the kettle on for us.

One day, I came in and I didn't go up to her. I went into the kitchen and ate a packet of biscuits. My sister was staying at my auntie's house. I hadn't seen her in weeks. I filled the kettle. I put my homework out on the table. I heard her on the stairs. I put the gas on under the kettle. I was holding my pen when she came in. I looked. It was my mother, not the other woman. Whatever I'd done — been a man — it had worked.

Rachel never told me why she'd cried. She stood behind me. I don't know if she read what I'd written. I don't remember what I wrote. There must have been a moment — a breakthrough, sometime after that night with Rachel — when I knew and accepted that I wasn't writing the book. It must have been quite like the moment when I knew that I was going to write it. I don't know.

Radio was fine. I went in there armed with other people's ideas. When I wrote, I had something of my own to write about. I was never lazy. Just inadequate. But I remember thinking — feeling — that by fucking Rachel I'd be up to anything. I'd be incisive, winning, brilliant. I believed in myself. And we were a match. I gave her something. I saw that the night she sat on the bed crying. I'm not sure what she saw. Some sort of solidity. Reliability. I was solid, or she'd decided that I was.

And we filled a gap. We were an outrageous couple. That claim seems daft today but that was what we were. We might have been Ireland's first celebrity couple. We were wild but together. A happily married couple who weren't actually married. (We never did get married. I started referring to Rachel as my wife after ten years or so. I couldn't say "girlfriend" any more and "partner", in our case, would have been confusing. Rachel, by then, had half a dozen partners.) We were unpredictable but she cooked and I wrote; she was in the kitchen and I was somewhere else in the building. Writing. Working on something. *He's cooking up something too, is he?* We were the celebrity couple but we were becoming well known for what we did alone. We were neck and neck, celebrity chef and your man on the radio. We made sense.

I remember waking, often, soon after my father died, and being unable to breathe. There was a rock, a boulder, on my chest. But I was awake and I'd sit back against the bedroom wall and the weight would be gone and my breathing went back to normal. Years later, when I heard my son breathe, when he was small and was having an asthma attack, I recognised the sound, the rhythm — the lack. Like he was pulling breath from a hole. I'd done the same. Until that stopped and I could lie down again. I don't remember being frightened. I was shocked that I was awake, the first time and maybe the second time. Somehow, I knew I should lean back against the wall. And leave my mother alone.

The loft was different. Because I didn't wake up. I *was* awake. Rachel was asleep beside me. I'd taken her book off the side of her face. She was reading *The*

175

Running Man. I'd kissed her hair, lowered the book to the floor. It was a hot night — August the 27th. We'd left two windows at the far end of the room open but the problem was the noise. We were living in Temple Bar. It was years before the madness but it was still Temple Bar. So the windows where we slept were shut. We'd only a sheet over us. Rachel had already kicked her share of it off. She was lying on her stomach. I was wide awake and didn't want to be. I didn't want to turn on the light, to read. I thought about writing something. I'd slip back into bed just when she was waking. She'd see the pages. I'd lay them on my chest, to make it look as if I'd dropped off, exhausted. It was what I wanted, honest exhaustion. Like hers. I pulled the sheet off me, shoved it to the end of the bed. I was turning — the pillow was too far back. My head — the side of my face — was down, a drop I hadn't expected because there was no pillow. It could only have been an inch but it felt like I was falling.

I think I hurt her. I must have. I exploded. I've nothing to describe it. No picture or sound. I burst apart. I stopped existing. But I knew exactly what had happened. When I was back again. When I knew she was beside me, holding on to me. And I didn't mind her hearing me cry.

— What happened?

I had no idea of time. How long there had been between lowering my head and hearing the fear in Rachel's voice.

— Victor?

I had to cry. It was the only way to drive it out of me. I could still feel the carpet. I could smell it. I could feel his hands. Pushing me down. Shoving my face.

He wasn't there. I was with Rachel. He wasn't there but he had been there and I had been there. I hadn't dreamt it — I'd been there. She leaned over me, across me; I could feel her nervousness. I could feel her shaking — I could see it — as she leaned across and turned on the light beside the bed.

— Okay? Victor — okay?

She tried to see my face.

— Okay?

I was still crying. I could feel the carpet, on the cheek that now lay against the sheet. I couldn't stop crying. I was pulling sludge — from somewhere under my lungs.

— It was a nightmare, she said.

I nodded, but then said No.

— No? she said.

I nodded again.

— What then?

She waited. She rubbed my back. She lay back down until she felt and saw me move. I lifted myself up, and back against the pillow. She helped — she straightened it behind my back. I wiped my eyes, my face.

— Sorry.

I let myself breathe; I let myself get it back to normal. I closed my eyes. I began to feel cold. It was a hot night but I was very cold. She lifted herself, and sat beside me. I told her. I told her what had happened to me. When I was fourteen, and just now. I didn't separate or join them. I just told her what had happened. A Christian Brother had pinned me to the floor and put his hands on my penis and testicles. The Head Brother, the principal of the school, had done that.

— Oh, Jesus.

— Yeah.

I wiped my face again and described the room, the floor, why I was there after school. How I'd ended up alone in the room with him.

— It wasn't my fault, I told her.

— What?

— It wasn't my fault, I said again.

— How can you say that?

— I wasn't the only one, I told her. — He taught us all how to wrestle.

— All of you?

— Some, I said. — A good few.

I told her more about the school. I told her about the Brother who'd fancied me in first year and about learning the Ó'Riada mass for the Brother who was dying. I told her about the stairs and the mad routes to the classrooms and the Virgin Mary with the hole in her back. I led her away from the Head Brother and me.

— It sounds dreadful, she said, but I knew I'd reassured her — and distracted her. I'd made a story of it.

In a few years, after we'd moved out of the loft, I started to meet men who'd ask me about school. We'd be sitting at the table in our house or at someone else's table, a friend or colleague of Rachel's.

— Which school did you go to, Victor?

Which? The possibilities were limited. There were only five or six schools I could have gone to, if I was one of them. The women always knew before the men: I wasn't one of them — they knew I was interesting. I'd come from another world, across the city.

— Nowhere you've heard of, I'd answer.

— Where?

— The Christian Brothers.

— Oh.

I didn't have to give the school a name or location. I might as well have told them I'd gone to school up the Limpopo. I'd start to talk. I'd tell them all about it. If we were at a table, all other chat would stop and they'd listen, appalled, delighted, spellbound.

— You should write about it.

— I am.

I'd start with the room, and being told to stay behind after the last bell. I'd tell them about the Head Brother.

— The fucking school principal?

— I'm not making this up.

— Sorry.

He asked me about my father; he knew my father was back in hospital. He asked how he was, how my mother was coping, if I was a support to her. *I'm sure you are.* We were all in his prayers, he told me, his and all the Brothers'. He knew I was going through a difficult time. He knew that, without my father at home, I was the man of the house and he was going to teach me how to defend myself. The rudiments, he said. The men at the table saw where I was going; the women were slower. I'd describe how it had been just that, at first. A lesson in wrestling moves, dealing with an attack. Strange but, in the world of the Christian Brothers, not all that strange. Then I told them that he put me on the floor and he was on top of me and his hand was on my crotch. Staying there. I couldn't get up. I didn't have permission to get up. It was the Head Brother, the principal of the school, who was holding me down.

— You just let him do it?

— Conor —!

There was nearly always one who wanted to blame me. I learnt to enjoy it.

— I was fourteen.

— Well — how small were you?

— Conor — for God's sake —

I stood up. I'm not a very big man.

— Smaller than I am now, I said.

I sat down again.

— I'd have fucking killed him, said Conor. — I'm sorry. I just know that if he'd —

He looked around at the other men.

— Did anything like that ever happen to any of us? he asked.

Us.

Most of them shook their heads. The others were worried that a shake of the head would propel me out of the room; they'd be denying the truth of what I'd just told them. They were nice people. Most of the women shook their heads too, often more vigorously than their husbands and boyfriends.

— The nuns were lovely.

180

I'd look across the table at Rachel. She'd smile. She knew. She'd seen me. She'd seen the truth. And she knew I was going to keep talking. She knew I was going to rescue them. Sometimes a question would get me moving again.

— Did it happen often?

— No, I'd say. — Only once. And look, it wasn't all bad.

And I'd tell them about the Brother sitting through his own funeral mass, and the Blessed Virgin and the art teacher with the paint-covered dog that barked when his master was battering a boy whose still life wasn't good enough, and the snot on the tip of the history teacher's nose, and the Brother who listened to Radio Luxembourg every night so he could tell us about God in the songs we'd been listening to the night before.

— So, it was just violence, really — the odd belt?

It would be Conor, or a version of Conor. Rachel worked with a lot of women who went out with the Conors; Rachel could have had her pick of the Conors. This one — the first one — was a rugby international. He was capped twice, I think. Before the knee. Everyone knew about the knee. He married a girl Rachel had gone to school with, who'd worked with her — for her — in the early Meals on Heels days. They'd actually met while she was working. It became a story people loved. They were interviewed together. *He put his hand on my bum*, she laughed. More phone calls to Rachel from mothers looking for part-time work for their daughters.

Only once, I told them. It had happened only once. That was true.

But it came back more than once, after that first time. Whatever it was. The Drop. That was what I named it.

— The Drop? Rachel would ask.

Always at night. Always lying down. Only in the loft. Only in those two years. She liked the name. It did the trick, caged it, made it comical. I don't know what I sounded like when it happened; I don't know how much of the place I invaded, if I jolted or kicked out. There was never blood or bruising. I never bit my tongue or hit out — I don't think I hit out. I never forgot that it had happened. I never quite lost the crawling feel across my skin, the feeling that I was going to be punched, kicked low. But its recurrence was always a shock. Weeks later — months later. I was on the floor in his office, the weight, the gasping. *Try to move now, Victor, try to move. What are you made of?* I didn't see the room. A patch of floor was all I got. The huge hand flattening me. Covering me completely. *Try to move — go on.* And I was looking at Rachel. She was standing beside the bed. I saw her see me. She sat on the bed as I sat back.

— It happened again, she said.

— Yeah.

— The same?

— I don't know.

And life went on.

Why the loft? Why only there, and only then? Now — today — I think it was because I was happy. I didn't

182

think that then. I couldn't have. I didn't know I was happy and I didn't know that happiness was finite.

I admit: I revealed it because I had nothing else to talk about. That was what I thought — I *knew* — at the time. I was going up the steps into the RTE radio centre, ready to nod at anyone coming out. It was raining and I hadn't a clue what I was doing there. I'd flicked through the papers in a newsagent's but nothing had stuck. Walking out of the shop, I'd already forgotten the headlines.

It had been a while since I'd received the call. Neither myself nor Rachel had mentioned it; I was working on the book. I was knuckling down. Nearly there. Year One, Year Two, Year Three. The phone had rung in the kitchen the night before. We'd both been there — a rare enough event, because Rachel was flying. Rachel was becoming Rachel. Rachel had become Rachel. I picked it up and listened to the producer. She was honest: the dancer who'd defected from the Soviet Union had cancelled his trip to Dublin, so would I come out for a quarter of an hour in the morning? I pretended to flick through my diary and told her I'd do it. I put the phone down and told Rachel.

— Great, she said.

She smiled and kept chopping the onions. And I got back to watching *Fireman Sam* with our son. And there I was the next morning, on the way down the stairs to the studios.

— Been to any gigs? the researcher asked.

— Not recently, I said.

— Any of the biggies grab you?

She meant the stories of the day. I still believed I'd be able to think of something. It was what I'd been believing for years. The pages would be filled and they'd be great. Rachel believed that too. She still looked at me, and held me, like I was the man she needed. She still referred to the spare room as my office, and she could do it without the hesitation and grin — the little quotation marks — that came later, before she stopped referring to it at all. I believed I'd come up with something that would fill the allotted time, that would get me invited back, that would allow myself and Rachel to grin whenever the phone rang just as we were putting the forks to our mouths or the plastic spoon to our son's.

The researchers had been my age once, or older. Now they were younger. This one was brand new.

— What I want to do, I told her, — is talk about something that happened to me when I was in school.

— Cool. What?

I told her.

— Wait there, she said.

I stood outside the studio door. I walked a few paces, came back, walked again, came back. I hadn't planned this. I was only now hearing what I'd said. If I had to wait I'd go, back up the stairs, out, home.

The studio door opened.

— Come in.

I went in, and looked through the studio glass. The producer was at Myles Bradley's ear. Literally at his ear. He was nodding. He didn't turn to look at her or through the glass, at me. No one said hello. Paper and control panels had never been studied so carefully. I could hear the ads. I always knew when they were coming to an end. I knew exactly when the producer would lift her head from the side of Myles's and come and get me — or stop me. I made sure I didn't pant, although I wanted to. I needed to. I needed air. I needed water. I needed to run. I needed her to see me, so I could shake my head and let her know that I'd changed my mind, that I hadn't really made the decision in the first place. She put her hand on the desk in front of her, and stood straight, and moved to the door. She was limping, or one of her legs was stiff. The door opened out.

— Did you hurt your leg? I asked her.

— Fell off my bike, she said. — Go on ahead. He's ready.

— Fine, I said.

— No names, she said.

I understood.

— Okay.

I passed her.

— Thank you, she said.

That got me the seven steps to the chair opposite Myles. He looked embarrassed, excited, scared. He glanced at me. He nodded, looked at the glass, listened, nodded again.

— Welcome back, he said.

He looked at me properly.

— Victor, he said. — Victor Forde. It's been a while. How are you?

— Well, thanks, I said.

— Am I right in thinking that the last time we spoke, it was about the schools?

— Probably, I said.

— Something about senior students and contraception, if I remember right.

— That sounds right, I said.

— You got the phones hopping — as usual.

— Sorry about that.

— Ah, now, said Myles. — That's a while back. But I remember thinking —

It was coming.

— And correct me if I'm wrong, Victor, said Myles. — But I remember thinking that school might not have been a good time for you. Am I right?

— It wasn't too bad, I told him.

— Is that right?

— Except —

— Yes?

— I went to a Christian Brothers school, I said.

A hand put a plastic cup of water in front of me. I held the cup — I didn't drink the water. But holding it seemed to be enough. The water was cold.

— Like so many of us, said Myles.

He shook his head, once, and mouthed two words: *Don't name.*

— It was okay, I said. — But.

I didn't say goodbye or thanks when I was finished. I had to get out. I had to vomit and shit. I was still in the

186

building — under the building — an hour after I'd stopped talking. In the toilet under the stairs. I don't know how many times I washed my hands and face. The corridor was empty when I came out.

I was walking along Morehampton Road, back into town, when I realised I didn't live in town. I remember smiling. I remember feeling good. And hungry now — starving. And I was terrified. He'd have heard it. The Head Brother would have heard it, or been told about it. All of this happened more than a quarter of a century ago but when it happened — when I spoke — I'd been out of school only twelve years or so. He was still out there, still teaching. And I was frightening him — and all of them. I stopped at a payphone but it was broken. The house was empty when I got home. Rachel was at work. Our son was at the crèche.

I stood at the fridge and ate everything in it that didn't need cooking, including three little pots of raspberry yoghurt and a bag of carrot sticks. I shut the fridge door. I stood in the kitchen. I was exhausted and restless — panicking. I stood at the stairs. I didn't go up. I thought I'd fall if I did. I'd smash my head on the corner of the dark-wood table I was standing beside now. I knew I'd fall. I felt elated too. Or, I wanted to feel elated. Then I thought of my mother. At home, listening to me on the radio.

The phone rang right beside me. I remember holding it — it was white and strangely warm. I mustn't have recited the number and said hello. I usually did that.

— Victor?

It was Rachel.

— Hi.

— You're home.

— Yeah.

— Why didn't you tell me? she said.

— What?

— I'd have stayed home, she said. — I'd have gone with you. Will I come home?

— Yes, I said.

— Will I?

— Yes.

I heard her talking to someone as she replaced the phone. I was sitting in the kitchen reading the paper when she came in. I heard the car, I heard the key in the door, heard her shoes on the cedarwood in the hall, onto the rug, back onto the wood. I looked up when I knew she was in the kitchen. She had bags in each hand. She was smiling. She was worried. And angry.

— Did you hear it? I asked.

— Most of it, she said. — I turned it on when I remembered you were on.

— They all heard?

I meant the women who worked with Rachel. She was still based in Temple Bar, although she'd been touring the industrial estates, looking for somewhere bigger.

— Yes, she said.

— And?

She came towards me and put the bags down. I saw vegetables, apples, a bag of basmati rice.

— They — , she said. — They were fine. I don't know — sympathetic? Moved. Why didn't you tell me?

— I didn't know.

— What?

— I didn't know I'd bring it up, I said. — This morning — when I left. I didn't know. I just decided.

— Victor.

— What?

— I'm proud of you.

I was sitting on one of the stools at the counter. She stood behind me and put her hands on my chest and stomach. She leaned against me.

— It won't be good for business, I suppose.

— Stop being stupid, she said.

I hoped she wouldn't notice my erection. And I hoped she would. I hoped she'd look for it.

— But why did you mention the other stuff? she asked.

— What do you mean?

She was still holding me, caressing me.

— The things you always do, she said. — The choir and the priest listening to his funeral.

— The Brother.

— The fucking Brother then. Listening to his own funeral music. Why did you?

— Why did I what?

— Well. Mention it. After —

— I wanted to be fair, I told her.

My account of the Brother molesting me had taken only three minutes. Some other presenter might have kept me on a straight line, but this was shocking stuff and Myles Bradley had had enough. And then, so had I. And I listened to myself, making small of it. Myles even had his own story to add: the day he mitched and went into a shop to buy sweets, only to discover his mother behind the counter; he'd forgotten she'd started work in the shop that morning. Eight minutes after I'd told Myles and the rest of Ireland that a Christian Brother had placed his hand on my penis, I was laughing.

But I'd told him, and I'd told them.

— Just to be clear, said Myles towards the end; I watched him looking through the studio glass. — This was just one Christian Brother we've been talking about.

—Yes.

— And it happened —?

— Once.

— Dreadful — but thank you. As ever, Victor, it's been a pleasure. We'll be right back.

Friends called — Rachel's friends called. I listened to her.

— He's fine.

Her sisters rang.

—Yes. No — I'm proud of him.

I took the phone from her each time.

— I'm fine. It's no big deal.

My mother rang.

—Why didn't you tell me?

— I should've — I'm sorry. And this morning — I should have warned you. But I — it wasn't planned. And it was no big deal. Mam. Honestly.

— Why didn't you tell me then? Victor, love. *Then.* Why didn't you?

— It happened to all of us, Mam.

— Rita Kelly told me it never happened to any of her lads. In the post office.

— It did, Mam. Believe me. But — look — don't be upset. It happened to everyone. Like an initiation. I forgot all about it until this morning. I'll be out to see you — yes — on Sunday.

All day, all night, I pushed myself back from what I'd said that morning. I heard it and tried to stop myself but it was too late.

There was uproar too. There was always uproar. I was undermining the Church and the education system; I was assaulting the country itself. I was a blackguard and a self-serving fuckin' little queer. Then, as it all calmed down, as I began to sleep again and venture from the house, there were those who nodded at me, one or two who shook my hand. Then I seemed to become the man who needed to hear the mitching stories and the Brothers were mad bastards stories. *I have one for you. Listen to this, you'll laugh.* I told Myles Bradley quite clearly that I'd been molested. But I'd kept talking. I should have stopped after I'd told him about the man's weight holding me down. I didn't exactly bury the story — *my* story — but I made it, somehow, an expected part of every Irishman's education. A bit of gas. Not so bad. Part of what we are.

I waited for a writ from the Brothers and I wondered why there hadn't been one. Then I got a call from a publisher. He was thinking of putting together a collection of people's memories of the Gaeltacht, for the Christmas market; would I be up to editing it? And I knew I'd lost something, again. A chance, my integrity — I don't know. Rachel was delighted when I told her about the job. I can remember her face. I hadn't seen that expression in a long time, and I only understood that now — now as I was looking at her. She agreed to give me a story of her own time in the Gaeltacht.

— What about you? she asked.

— What?

— Will you write something too?

— I never went to the Gaeltacht, I told her.

— Did you not?

— No.

— How come?

I shrugged.

— Just didn't, I told her. — Anyway, the editor should never include anything he's written himself. It's not the thing.

I didn't tell her that the boys in my school always went to the Brothers' own college in Spiddal, and that the Head Brother would have been on the bus west with them. I could have written about the boy I'd been then. *Why I Didn't Go to the Gaeltacht.*

CHAPTER
THIRTEEN

—You woke me.

— Did I? How?

— Victor.

— What?

— You texted me. Last night.

— Did I?

— Yes.

— But what —

— Don't ask me what you bloody said, Victor. Look it up, yourself.

I was worried now. Had I flung a bunch of texts at her? I couldn't check them while I was still talking to her.

— Sorry, I said. — I had a few last night.

— That's not like you, she said.

There was no edge to the words, no concern. She could have been reading them out.

— I was with some friends, I told her. — We made a night of it.

— Sounds good, she said.

— What did I say?

— I'm writing, exclamation marks — two of them. And two "x"s. To be exact.

— Well, it's true, I said. — I am writing.

I tasted the words in my mouth.

— Should I be worried? she asked.

— Very.

I was flirting, or trying to — and trying not to.

— How are you? she asked.

— Fine — yeah. You?

— Okay, she said. — The usual.

Tell me about the usual. I'll listen this time.

— So, she said. — I'm glad you're writing, Victor. But there's no need to text me every time you pick up a pen or whatever.

— I was just — sorry. Excited, I suppose.

— And drunk.

—Yeah. But I was using that notebook you gave me.

— What notebook?

—You gave me a notebook.

— I gave you dozens of them, Victor.

—Well, I can only use one at a time. In fairness.

She was smiling — I knew. It was one of our phrases. "In fairness". A "do". We'd collected them, together. I could have added another — "by the way". *I love you, by the way.*

I could see her as she said goodbye. Nothing stopped when Rachel was on the phone. Before mobiles, I'd seen her standing beside a desk, using her free hand and her eyes, an orchestra conductor; her people flowed around her. The thing — the performance — was flawless, graceful, always clear. And gorgeous. I could see her now, although I hadn't a clue where she was when we were talking. I'd asked her, but she hadn't told me. But I could see her, giving me her attention, and sending an assistant out of the room, inviting a scriptwriter in, demanding that flowers be moved to a place beside an open window, drawing circles around ingredients and sending the list on its way, nodding and shaking her head as her tall minions passed her — always the smile, the slightly lopsided smile, the proof that she was and she wasn't perfect; always the sense that this was a dance, a well-rehearsed performance, that she'd anticipated the spilt coffee — Rachel drank black coffee, and she called it "black coffee" — and the late arrival of the cameraman and the fainting intern; nothing was unexpected, nothing was truly unwelcome. She was checking on me, making sure I was alright, going through the duties of an ex-wife with an unhinged, disappointing ex-husband, letting me know that I was loved, that I was needed, while she approved the studio make-up that had been applied while she spoke, or made sure her studio chair was at exactly the right angle, or a designer held a tablet in front of her and flicked through logo options, or she lay back on the bed in what had been our bedroom and smiled up at her lover as she told me she was glad I was writing, or. Or. Or. Or.

CHAPTER
FOURTEEN

Fitzpatrick was standing beside the cigarette machine — the bulk of him, the shorts, the pink shirt. He looked different, a bit lost, none of the flat-faced boom he'd pushed at me before. I was still at the door. He hadn't seen me. The cigarette machine was off in a corner. His pint of Heineken was on top of it.

I made my move. The men were near a window, at one of the high tables. Harry wasn't there but there was another man I'd seen with them before. I headed to the bar, and One Direction standing behind the taps. I looked around, and Pat was looking at me.

— Ready for another? I asked.

He looked into his pint, then looked back at me and nodded. I showed One Direction four fingers. He nodded and got busy.

— Is Harry here? I called across, in case I needed to order another pint.

Pat shook his head. Fitzpatrick had probably seen me by now. I didn't look his way. I took out my phone and stared at it. I looked at the progress of the pints. There were two settling, two being poured. I took out my twenty euro and left it on the bar, and went across to the window. I nodded at the new guy.

— How's it going?

— Not too bad.

— Did you get caught in the fuckin' rain earlier? Pat asked.

He was up on a stool, back to the window. He always seemed to get the stool.

— No, I said. — I was working.

It was true — it felt true. I'd done a bit before I'd come out. A page a pint, I'd decided.

— The young lad is waving at you, said Liam.

I turned, and the kid was standing behind a line of four pints. I took two of them and the change.

— Good man; thanks very much.

I carried the pints across to the window. *How's it going? Good man; thanks very much.* The words felt great and a bit forbidden. I hadn't earned the right to slip into the rhythm of the middle-aged Dub. My father had liked a pint, my mother told me. He'd liked the company of other men. Maybe that was me. A late arrival.

— Here we go.

— Good man.

I went back up for the other two pints. I glanced across; Fitzpatrick wasn't at the cigarettes. He might have gone roaming. I suspected now that he had three or four locals; small doses of himself in each. I thanked the kid again and went back to the table. The woman, Brenda, was there. I had to lean across slightly to get a pint to Pat. I brushed against her. She was wearing something that looked like a polo-neck scarf; I felt it on the inside of my arm.

— Sorry.

She turned and saw me, and smiled.

— Ah, hiya.

— Hi.

— I was just telling the lads, she said. — I got drenched earlier.

— That must have been dramatic, I said.

I felt a bit brave, and stupid.

She examined me — she examined the words before she smiled.

— Go 'way, you messer, she said.

I took a step away from her and stood beside the new guy — the new guy who'd been coming here for decades before I'd walked in.

— No Harry tonight, I said.

— The wife's birthday.

— Ah.

— Poor fucker, he said. — Nice meal, good bottle of wine, a good ride from one of the better-looking women in the locality. And he could be here with us.

— My heart goes out to him, I said.

— He's in my fuckin' prayers. I'm Martin, by the way.

— Victor.

— Yeah.

We watched Brenda depart.

— D'you remember her when she was in school? said Liam.

— I fuckin' do, said Pat.

I looked at Martin and he half looked back at me.

— I still would, said Pat.

198

— We all would, said Martin.

They'd been saying the same thing for years. I was in there too now. I'd never been happier. That isn't true. But it felt true. I could see the building site across the road, over the pebbled lower pane of the window.

— A bit strange, I said. — Isn't it? A building site. After all these years.

— It is, Liam agreed. — I'd forgotten things got built. Pat nodded at Martin.

— His game.

— You're a builder? I asked.

Martin nodded.

— Is that one of yours?

I meant the site across the way.

— No, he said. — Fuck, no. Unfortunately.

— Are things really picking up? I asked.

I wondered — for a second — if there was an article there, an interview with a small-time builder. How he'd managed for the last seven years. It crossed my mind, and left.

— Definitely, he said.

— What are they building over there?

— Apartments.

I'd look at them, I decided. I wouldn't be able to afford one, but I'd look. I'd figure out how much I'd have to earn, what I'd have to do. Could a man of my age even get a mortgage? I'd find out. Football, *Game of Thrones*, holiday plans, retirement plans, Robin Wright, craft beer, college fees, Nick Cave. It could have been any of the nights I had ahead of me. I felt it again: I'd never been happier. Four pints — click — we stood up to go home.

It wasn't that night, it was another night, the next night, when I knew there was someone behind me. There'd been four of the men, the full contingent, so I'd had five pints. I could feel the weight of the extra pint and all the pints. I was drunk. I think I was counting the steps from gate to gate, enjoying the rhythm and the slap of my feet. The trees had taken over the street — they seemed to do this at night-time. I had to duck to avoid some of the branches. I was nearly there. *Five pints, five pints, five pints, five pints.* It would have been new for the men too — that occurred to me. I was the extra pint, not Harry or Martin. I wondered if they were talking about that. If they were cursing the fact that they'd let me in.

There was someone behind me, nearly on my heels. I thought of Fitzpatrick; he hadn't been in the pub. I thought of him first, and I turned. But I knew it was a woman — the heels, the pace. I knew it was Brenda before I saw her.

— God, she said. — You go at a fair clip.

She'd walked into me. She was a bit drunk too. She was right into me and my hands were on her shoulders. She stepped back and I took my hands away. I liked her height. She was different. She wasn't Rachel. She was fattish and human. And curious. And probably unhappy. And mad.

— I didn't know you lived down this way, she said.

— Yeah, I said. — I'm in one of the apartments.

— Oh. What're they like?

— Not too bad, I said. — They're better than they look from the outside. Mine is, anyway.

— Good.

We walked beside each other — or tried to.

— You live down here too, obviously, I said.

— Well, I'm not following you, she said. — If that's what you're thinking.

She had that combination of come on and fuck off. It was years since I'd banged into it.

— Never occurred to me, I said. — There are limits to my imagination.

— Go 'way out of that, she said. — Are you living on your own in there?

— That's it, I said. — All on my own.

— I wouldn't like that, she said.

— It's not too bad.

— It might be different for men.

— It might be. What about you?

— What about me?

— The domestic arrangements.

— Four bedrooms, two toilets, three kids, the dog, an occasional cat, one husband, and a mobile home in Cahore.

I laughed. We were at the railings and the gate to the car park. There was a cat sitting beside one of the wheelies.

— Is that one yours? I asked.

— No, she said. — Much more meat on our lad. Do they go in and out?

— The cats?

— Yeah. Into the apartments, like.

— Not that I've seen, I said. — They stay out here. And around the back.

— They give me the creeps.

— Me too, I said. — A bit. But I kind of like them as well. D'you want to come in?

— No.

She smiled.

— No.

I wasn't disappointed. I was probably relieved. I was too drunk for any activity that involved precision or listening. I didn't want to sit beside her and think that I'd soon have to get up and go for a piss.

— But d'you know what? she said. — It's nice to be asked.

She held my arm. She stepped in and kissed me on the cheek.

— I'll keep asking, so, I said.

— Do, she said.

I got into the flat. I went to the window, pulled back the curtain. I looked left, to see if I could spot Brenda on her way home. I opened the window, pushed it out — the hinge complained — and listened for her heels. Heard nothing like heels. I left the window open. I liked the wind in the branches, the odd car door slamming, a shout from up on the main road, a siren miles away. Music from above. A thump-thump-thump I didn't have a name for — a band, a genre, I hadn't a clue. There was someone on the other side of the street. Walking past. A man, a big guy. It was hard to see through the shadows and low branches. There was a gap in the trees, where there were two wide driveways side by side. He walked from behind the tree, across the gap. Fitzpatrick. He walked like he was listening to the music above me. Thump thump thump. He looked like a big kid on his way home from football. He didn't slow down, he didn't look back.

I saw him again. A few days later. Early morning — bright, but very quiet — it was just after six. I'd stayed at home the night before. I was wide awake and restless. I saw him. Down the street. He'd been crossing it, from my side. I saw the pink back, the shorts, before he went behind the trunk of a hundred-year-old tree. It was him. On his way home.

A taxi slid in from the opposite direction. It stopped, stalled. It wasn't dark but the indicator lit the air under the trees. A girl got out. The girl I'd seen before. She shut the back passenger door. She didn't let it slam. She had her shoes in one hand, her bag in the other. She walked across the car park. She walked carefully over the car-park stones. I looked for Fitzpatrick. He wasn't there.

— Are you going to come up?

I saw her decide; I hoped she'd change her mind. I hoped she wouldn't.

It was later that same day, the day I'd seen Fitzpatrick crossing the street.

— Yes, she said. — Okay. For a while, just.

I led the way across the car park. I'd slowed, to let her walk beside me. But she didn't seem to want that. This was big; this was her street, her neighbours, her life. I didn't feel drunk, or too drunk. I stopped hearing her steps on the stairs. I turned — I held the banister.

— I don't know, she said.

She was halfway up the stairs.

I didn't answer.

— I've to be up in the morning, she said.

I was willing to be rejected.

— Okay, I said. — Another time.

— Just a quick cuppa, she said.

She followed me up and stood back while I opened the door. I half hoped she'd change her mind again. And I didn't. I wanted to put my hands on her back. I wanted to kiss the skin between her shoulder blades.

She closed the door with a little click. It really was a crummy place. The sad nest of a new, forced bachelor. But it wasn't. I knew: every happily married man and woman wanted a place just like this.

We were five feet apart.

— You're my first guest, I told her.

— I'm honoured, she said.

She smiled. She put hair behind an ear. She glanced at the other two doors.

— We'd better celebrate, I said. — I've no beer, or wine — sorry. Tea or Bovril?

— D'you have Bovril?

— No.

— I haven't had Bovril in years, she said. — I used to like a mug of Bovril.

— Is this where we're at? I asked, as I filled the kettle. — Two secret lovers talking about Bovril.

She laughed.

— We're not lovers — excuse me.

— And we've no Bovril.

She sat down on the couch. I sat beside her.

— A cuddle'll do me, she said.

— Me too.

— I can't stay.

— Grand.

— Like — I don't want to stay.

— Fine.

— What's she like?

— Who?

— Rachel, of course. Your Rachel.

— The man himself, he said.

We were in SuperValu. *I* was in SuperValu and he was suddenly right beside me, bang up against me. I'd just opened a high fridge door, to get at a carton of cream of tomato soup. I noticed the pink cloud — the shirt — in the fridge glass before I knew it was him. I thought I was being pushed in, I thought I was being robbed. He was vast, away from the shadows of the pub. His feet were apart because they had to be. There was a grass stain on one leg of his shorts.

— Doing the shop, he said.

— Yep.

— Same as meself.

— A pain in the arse, I said.

He looked in my basket. There was brown bread in there, and apples, and flat peaches.

— You're looking after yourself, anyway, he said. — I've seen you with your new buddies.

I tried to think of something to say. He didn't push, but I had to get out of his way as he leaned in and took down the soup that I'd been aiming at. He looked at it — he actually stared at the carton and tossed it back up on its shelf.

— Did you tell them yet? he said.

— Tell them what?

— About the Brother playing with your mickey.

There was no one else near us. I stepped back out of his heat.

— Don't start, I said.

— Start what? he said. — Start what? I thought it was your fuckin' party piece.

I wanted to walk but I was afraid he'd thump the back of my head, kick the back of my leg, trip me up, drop on me. I was afraid.

— I'm only messing with you, he said.

He smiled. He shrugged. He didn't have a basket. He didn't have anything. He'd followed me. And I remembered him then — the shrug, the grin; I remembered the boy inside the bulk. I thought I did.

— The fucker got to all of us, he said. — He went right through the fuckin' roll book. Are you going down tonight?

I didn't know what he meant at first.

— What?

— Are you going to the pub? Hello —?

— I don't know —

— Will I call for you? he said. — I know where you live.

The grin was back.

206

— Don't mind me, he said. — I'm just acting the prick. Go on ahead with your shopping.

He didn't move. I had to do it. It took effort, decision. I wasn't sure how I walked away.

I kept going.

— See you later, he shouted.

I shouted too.

— Okay.

He was waiting for me, standing between me and the men. I'd stayed away the night before, after I'd seen him in SuperValu. But I wasn't going to stay away for good. I liked what I was starting to have. Friends. Banter. Brenda. I'd put up with him; I'd have to. I'd accommodate him, roll with him. I couldn't spend my time looking out the window, half expecting to see him in the trees. I couldn't be scared of him.

I bought him a pint when I was buying my own. I'd chat to him, give him the bit of attention, then I'd move across to the men. If he came with me, fine; I'd bring him. They could deal with him. He'd been a fixture in the pub for years. I put his Heineken in front of him, on the counter. My pint was settling.

— Do you remember the last day? I asked him. — I was thinking about it a few days ago.

— What last day?

— Last day of school, I said.

— Jesus, he said. — The land before fuckin' time.

— There was — I don't know. I suppose, a reception. A do. Us and all the teachers, and the Brothers. In the hall.

— What hall?

— The new hall they built.

— It wasn't a hall, he said.

— It was.

— No.

— Where the tea and cakes were. It was — it was definitely in the hall.

— Sports complex.

— Was that what they called it?

— Yep.

— Christ.

— Four walls and a fuckin' roof.

— I hated it, I said.

— School?

— Yeah.

He stared at me, and shrugged.

— Can you remember who told the Head Brother to fuck off? I asked him.

He stared at me again. But it was actually hard to know if he was staring. It was as if he turned off for a second or two in mid-look.

— The last day, I said. — Before the Leaving. Do you remember?

— Yeah, he said eventually.

I'd looked across at the men while I was waiting for him to answer.

— Am I fuckin' detaining you? he said.

I looked at him properly.

— No.

— Grand. That was me.

— What?

— I told the fucker to fuck off.

— It was you?

— I told you — yeah. It was me.

I'd been thinking about that day, thinking about working some version of it into the story — the novel — I was writing. I could hear the words, the voices. I could see a path opening. I remembered that — people getting out of the way. The words tumbling down the passage ahead of him, the silence closing in after him. The sun coming through the window glass high up on each of the walls. But I couldn't see him. I couldn't see Fitzpatrick storming out.

— It was you? I said.

— Yep.

— Why?

He let go of some breath. He shrugged.

— Why not?

— Did you plan on saying it? I asked.

— Are you fuckin' serious? he said. — I never planned a thing in my fuckin' life.

He slapped my shoulder, hard.

— That's my fuckin' problem.

His eyes were wet as he laughed.

— What fuckin' consequences!

I laughed with him. I didn't want to leave him alone. There was something raw there, open in front of me.

— Did you do the Leaving after that? I asked him. — Did they let you?

— You don't remember.

He was staring at me again.

— I do, but —

— Fuck the Leaving, he said. — Enough of that shite. Life's too fuckin' short. What do you think of Brenda?

— What?

— Fuck off now. I have eyes, you know. The walls have fuckin' ears. She's a great knitter, you know. House full of fuckin' wool. She'd knit here if she could get away with it. They all would. The sexy oul' ones over there.

He clapped his hands.

— Fuckin' great, he said.

I laughed. There was something about him, something I'd been trying to avoid. I was liking him.

— Come here, he said. — Did you ever get a tug from a woman that knits? You probably have.

— No.

— No?

— I don't know.

— Oh, you would, he said. — Believe me. Nothing like it. No supermodel could come close to a fifty-year-old bird that knits. Ask Brenda. She'll demonstrate it for you.

He wasn't being quiet; he didn't care.

— Has to be real wool, mind. Fuck the synthetic fibres.

He wasn't offering to get us the next round. I was drinking more since I'd met the other men; I was able to. It was strange, but that made me feel fitter. I looked across at them.

— Am I keeping you? he said again.

—We might as well go over, I said.

I took what was left of my pint. I knew he'd follow. I'd buy the next round and include him. He'd be getting two pints out of me. I'd been leaving the flat with an extra twenty euro in my pocket, just in case. I was running out of money. It was Thursday night and the place was busy, the way I'd begun to like it. All four were in — Harry, Martin, Pat, Liam. I put my glass down carefully among the other glasses. I nodded at the table and the glasses.

— We ready?

— Stupid question.

— Go on ahead.

I turned to Fitzpatrick, but he hadn't followed me. He was standing where we'd been, staring down at his phone. I went back over, smiled at one of Brenda's pals on the way. I could tell: she didn't know. And there'd been no swapped looks from the men. No one knew about myself and Brenda. So, how had Fitzpatrick known?

— D'you want a pint? I asked him.

He was slow bringing his eyes, and his head, up from the screen. His back was fully straight before he turned his head to look at me.

— Yeah.

One of the lounge girls was at the counter. I gave her the order, five pints of Guinness and a pint of Heineken, and pointed to where I wanted them delivered.

— Perfect, she said.

Fitzpatrick had gone back to his phone.

— You coming over? I asked him.

He looked up, then back down, without looking at me.

— No, he said. — Go on.

I took the Heineken off the lounge girl's tray and handed it to him. He said nothing. I said nothing. I waited, hesitated, a second, two seconds, then went. I'd been watched.

— What's up with your man? said Liam.

— Well, I said. — You know, yourself.

— No.

— Who is he, anyway? Pat asked.

There was glee in the question. The others weren't as eager but they all wanted the answer. But the question had knocked me.

— I thought you knew him, I said.

I looked at them. I looked at Harry, hoping he'd nod, smile — I wasn't sure why. Things were suddenly missing. I felt dizzy, as I sometimes did when I stood up too quickly.

— No, said Pat.

— Like, we've seen him around, said Liam. — In here. And around.

— Ed, said Martin. — That's his name, isn't it?

— Yeah, I said. — Fitzpatrick. I went to school with him.

— Is that it? said Martin. — I thought you might be cousins or something.

— No, I said. — I hardly know him. Just when we were kids. Actually — he introduced us.

— Introduced?

— Over there, I said, and I nodded at the bar. — When we met.

I looked, but Fitzpatrick was gone.

★ ★ ★

She liked the adventure, she liked being a bit scared. She liked to think that she was tiptoeing along a cliff edge, that her husband would care. But she liked me too. And I liked her.

She leaned out and took up her tea.

— It's silly, she said. — But you kind of expect famous people to be a bit obnoxious.

— Why?

— Because they can be, she said.

She sipped from the mug.

— Would you be like that? I asked her.

— If I was famous?

— Yeah.

— Famous for what? Driving the kids to school?

— I'd say you excel at it, I said.

— Driving the kids?

— Yeah.

— You're gas.

— But just imagine you're famous, I said. — Would you misbehave — be obnoxious?

— God, yeah.

— Really.

— Oh, yeah.

— But really.

— Yes!

She sat up. She turned to me. She tucked her legs in under herself, grabbed a foot and pulled it into place. Her eyes were lit — young, sober, full of a kid's fun.

— I would love to send the food back in a restaurant and not feel like a tit. Did Rachel do that?

— Once.

— Only once?

— That I saw.

— Or I'd love to be able to say, *Do you know who I am?* I would so love that. That bitch in the chemist's. When she asks me if the Nurofen is for myself. I'd look her up and down and — *Do you know who I am?* And she wouldn't dare say No. I'd shove the sugar barleys and the Fisherman's Friends off the counter.

— Off you go.

— I've thought about this, she said. — I have; it's mad. And I know. I wouldn't let myself enjoy it. I'd apologise and help her pick the stuff up off the floor. And tell her her blouse is lovely. Was Rachel not a bitch even sometimes?

— No.

— Really?

— Not that I can remember.

— You're just being loyal.

— No.

— You still love her, don't you?

I wasn't walking along any kind of a precipice.

— Yeah, I told her. — I do.

She put her hand on my leg. She took it away and patted my cheek.

— What's your husband like? I asked.

— Why do you want to know?

— I don't know, I said. — Balance. You ask about my wife.

— Yeah, but I actually do want to know about Rachel. You couldn't give a toss about Dave.

214

— Go on, I said. — He's called Dave.

—Yeah, and he's grand, she said. — A bit of a prick, but grand.

— He's never in the pub, is he?

—Weekends, just. Sometimes. He works in England, did I never tell you?

— I think — maybe. Yeah, I think you did.

— Yeah, she said. — Six years now. He could move back. There's work again now. If he really wanted to. But — Next year. Next year. Next year. The prick.

— Sorry.

—That's why I don't feel too bad about this.

— Revenge.

— I wish.

She fought her unhappiness. She sometimes won, and it was lovely to watch. She leaned in and kissed me. She kept her mouth closed. She put a hand on each of my thighs. We were fully dressed. She was looking straight at me. The lights were off, just the candle I'd lit on the table behind us. She'd brought the candle the last time she'd come up to the flat. I could see her clearly. Her eyes were brown. I'd remember that. It seemed important. It seemed good.

—What did she see in you? she asked.

She wasn't slagging me or being sardonic, or working herself up to escape. She was asking herself a question.

— I think I know, she said. —You're nice.

I didn't expect it. I didn't believe it. But I liked hearing it and I didn't deny it.

— Thanks, I said.

— Am I? she said. — Nice as well.

— Yes, I said. — You are.

I went back out with her ten minutes later, when she was going home. I hadn't done that before. I'd sometimes wondered how she felt going down the stairs, across the car park, up the street — past windows, taxis, tired men putting out the wheelies. I'd watched her from my window; I'd pushed back the curtain to see her. She didn't rush, she didn't hesitate before she stepped from the car park onto the street. But a woman alone, a middle-aged woman walking alone at half one in the morning — it looked interesting, strange, a story. Maybe she wanted that. Maybe she liked the story. Maybe she just wanted me to put my hands on her three times a week, she wanted me to laugh at her jokes, to laugh at mine. To feel a man her age getting hard when she held him. Maybe she just wanted to know what Rachel was like. Or to sit close to the man who'd once sat close to Rachel.

She went down the stairs slightly sideways, and slowly. She got to the ground floor and stopped.

— Why are you following me?

It wasn't really a question. She enjoyed the whispering.

— Just seeing you to the door, I said.

— Suddenly you're a gentleman.

— Something like that.

I got to the front door before her and pulled it open, tried not to let it screech, and failed.

— Drop of oil needed there, she said.

— There's something wrong with the frame, I said.

She went out. I followed, caught up with her.

— Not all the way home, please, she said.

— No.

— Don't get weird on me.

— To the path, just.

— Okay.

She grabbed my hand and squeezed it, and let go. We stopped at the gate. She lifted herself the bit she needed to and kissed me, pushed me back and nearly tripped. We held one another to steady ourselves, and laughed lightly.

— See you when I see you, she said.

I watched her go, one tree, two trees, then turned back in. The cats were watching.

— Fuck off, I whispered. — Go on.

I took the steps up two at a time. Because I could. Because I wanted to. Because it captured something in me that night. I'd left the door on the snib. I was in and taking my trousers off before I sensed — I knew — there was someone in the room.

— The trousers come off after the bird leaves. Doesn't make fuckin' sense.

He was behind the curtain. That was what I thought at first. I'd left the light off but the candle was still burning. I couldn't see him. I hadn't seen him. I'd imagined it. But there'd been too many words. I'd heard them and now I saw him. He was right in front of me and his fist — a fist, a huge fist — went straight into me, into my face. It didn't stop, it went right in, impaled me to the air.

I wasn't there any more, I wasn't there.

I was sitting — I'd fallen back. I was trying to push myself over the back of the couch. To get away, to wake up. I tasted blood. Fitzpatrick was standing over me and he'd never looked bigger.

— Right, he said.

Just that.

— Right.

I could see him breathing, filling the room.

— Right.

His breath was mine. I could feel the breath being pulled from me. Through the blood. With the blood. He was taking in my breath, pulling it into himself. He creaked. He moved. He moved away from over me. He moved back. The back of his leg shoved the coffee table aside. Brenda's mug fell over. Brenda, Brenda. This was about Brenda. But he wasn't Dave, the husband. He was Fitzpatrick. In the shorts and pink shirt, and my hoodie. He was sitting on the coffee table and he was staring at me.

—You think I'm a joke, don't you?

I understood nothing. I was afraid to touch my face. I was afraid to breathe too deep, afraid of the damage that would announce itself — loose teeth, exposed nerves, broken nose. I sipped air. He was staring at me. I don't know how long it stayed that way. I didn't move. He didn't move. My teeth were okay. I thought I could speak. I thought I'd done well; I hadn't rushed into words. I'd accepted what was here. Fitzpatrick. In my flat. He'd attacked me. He was sitting on the coffee table, in front of me. He had me trapped. I thought I knew why.

— We didn't do anything, I said.

He shifted slightly, creaked again.

— I beg your pardon?

— We didn't do —

— Who's we?

— Brenda.

— Brenda?

There was a deep, terrible second. I thought he was growing in front of me. His feet, his knees, were moving closer. His knees were like plates, fists.

— What didn't you do? he said.

There'd be no good answer, no escape. He was going to come at me again.

— Go on, he said. — Tell us.

— Nothing.

— Nothing? he said. — That's about right.

He stayed still, there. He literally didn't move.

— You didn't ride her.

— No.

— Sorry? Say again.

— No.

— No. You didn't.

— It was just —

— What?

— Friendship.

— Friendship? he said. — Fuckin' friendship?

I expected him to laugh or to snort. But he didn't. He didn't do anything. I wondered again if it was happening. If he was really in front of me. If I was on the couch. Too frightened to move, to take back my room. Too deeply asleep to push him away.

— Okay, he said. — Here's how it is. I was riding her, myself. Sorry — I'm being disrespectful. Brenda and myself were in a relationship and then you came along.

Now it made sense and now I could get angry. I didn't mind being beaten; I had it coming. But I'd hit back. I'd hurt him.

— Nothing too formal, he said. — A bit like yourselves. Except a bit more than — for fuck sake now, Victor — *friendship*. But anyway, that's why I'm here. To beat the living fuck out of you. Because you stole my bird off me.

He still didn't move.

— My fat bird, he said. — My MILF. With a fanny as wide as O'Connell Street. The widest street in Europe, by the way.

He sounded like he was reading the words in bad light, alone. There was no energy in them.

— No, he said. — Sorry, Victor.

He creaked.

— It's not as easy as that, he said. — I wish it was. Believe me.

— I don't have any money, I said.

— Ah Jesus, Victor. Just fuckin' stop.

— Why are you here?

— Guess.

— No.

— Go on — guess.

— Fuck off.

The idea of hitting him was ridiculous. I wanted him to charge at me.

— I am you.

I thought I'd heard the words. But I couldn't grab them; there were other words I hadn't heard.

— Was it school? I asked.

He didn't move.

— Did I do anything to you?

I noticed it now. One of his legs was twitching. The noise followed, and I realised that it had been there for a while. A rasping sound — his shorts were rubbing against the edge of the coffee table. He was always restless. There was always something moving. A leg, a hand, his head. He was always looking around him, slapping himself, bouncing on his toes, rubbing a knee or his hands. This was definitely Fitzpatrick. He hadn't answered my question.

— Was it school?

— Think, he said.

— I am.

— Think.

— About what?

— School.

— What about it?

He stood. He shook himself; that was what I seemed to be seeing. He sat again. The candle flickered. It was going to die. He was still again.

— What about school? I asked.

— Concentrate, he said. — Go on — fuckin' concentrate.

— I'm trying.

I hated my voice.

— Well, you're shite at it, he said. — Pure shite. I am you.

— What do you mean?

I was shaking now, like him. There was something — something else — creeping up on me. It wasn't in the room. But it was there.

— School, Victor, he said. — Tell me one thing we did together in school.

— We weren't really friends —

— More friends, he said. — What is it about you and friends, Victor? What is it you're fuckin' clinging to? Think now and tell me. One thing we did together, me and you.

I waited.

— Good man, he said. — You're thinking.

I wasn't. I already knew the answer.

— Nothing, I said. — We didn't do anything.

— That's right, he said. — We never sat beside each other, even.

— You weren't in my school, I said.

— I was.

— You weren't.

There wasn't one memory, not a glimpse of him. He wasn't there. He wasn't with the lads, in among them or on the edge. He wasn't in the classroom. He wasn't laughing or crying, sitting at the back, standing at the front. He wasn't in there. I'd never known him.

— What about telling the Head Brother to fuck off? I asked him.

— What about it?

— Was that you?

He shrugged. I saw his shoulders, two blunt mountains, move.

— Was it *you?* he said.

— No.

— You sure about that?

I leaned over the arm of the couch and vomited. The tea I'd drunk with Brenda, the pints, the lasagne, the lies, the gaps, the facts, the bits of my life fell out in a second.

I straightened up — I sat back up.

— What are you doing? I asked him. — What do you want?

— Come here, he said.

He was twitching again. The shake had passed up from his leg. He nodded across at the table and my laptop. Just as the candle went out.

— The stuff you've been writing in there, he said. — Fuckin' hell.

— You read it?

— 'Course I did. Calm down. It's not bad either. But it's all about sex, isn't it? Mad stuff. Reminded me of when I was fifteen or something. When everything gave you the horn, d'you remember? 'Course you do. You're the writer. The fuckin' author.

His right leg was moving to the beat of the words. I could hear it and just about see it.

— Then Brenda, he said.

He'd thrown me. School, then back to half an hour ago. I had to think, to remember Brenda.

— There's your chance, he said. — The leg-over. A real one now, fuck the laptop. But you don't.

— No, I said. — It's like I said.

— She's not a bad-looking bird, he said.

— No, I agreed.

— In her own right, he said. — Can you not manage it?

It was a real question. He was curious.

— Can you wank? he asked.

— Yes.

— I can't.

He was — he was devastated. He'd cut himself open in front of me. I couldn't see him clearly but the hurt was in the words.

— Why not? I asked.

— Think.

— This isn't fair, I said.

— Well, Victor, he said. — You got that one right. Well done, you. It's not fair. It's never been fair. Have you tried the Viagra?

— No.

— Okay, he said. — I often wondered.

— What?

— If it worked. Always, like. In all cases.

— School, I said.

— Good man, he said. — Back to the subject. You know what I like about you, Victor?

— What?

— You always know where you're going — you seem to. You have that thing about you. I've seen you — you always look like you're going somewhere, you know what you're doing.

— I don't —

— Not the point, Victor. You look like it. You have something to do — important. To you, like. I'm not slagging you or anything. I'm being serious. You have that purpose. That thing. Where did you get that?

— I don't know.

— But you know what I mean?

— I think so.

— I never —

He sighed — contracted, grew again.

— I see people walking, he said. — Just during the day, like. I see them and they all seem to know where they're going. And I always think they're keeping the secret from me. Where they're going — where they know they're going. I've always felt that. Left out, I suppose. Excluded — that's a big word these days, isn't it, Victor? Excluded.

He stopped. He shifted slightly. I thought he was searching for something in a pocket.

— I was a happy enough kid, he said. — Remember?

— No.

— You do, he said. — But I always felt a bit left out — left behind. It was always hard work.

He clapped his hands. I jumped. I felt puke in my mouth again.

— But I was happy enough, he said. — Until that fuckin' cunt got his hands on me.

I could see his eyes.

— Remember?

— Yes.

— Yes, he said. — You do.

— I have to — I need to go to the toilet.

— Shit where you're sitting, he said.

— Please.

— No, he said. — You're grand. Take a breath. You remember. You know what I'm talking about.

— The Head Brother.

— Yeah. You remember alright. You made your living remembering. You went on the radio and told the whole world about it.

— What?

— The Brother — the cunt. What he did to us.

— I didn't know he did it to you.

— You did.

— I didn't. I don't even remember you.

— Do you want to be slapped again, do you?

He hit me before he'd finished, slapped me. He waited until he'd stopped panting, until I'd stopped panting, and he spoke again.

— I'm you, you fuckin' eejit.

— What?

— I'm —

— No — what do you mean?

— Exactly what I said. Literally what I said. No escape, Victor. I am you.

— That doesn't make sense.

— It does, you know. If you think about it.

His right leg was going again.

— But that's the thing, he said. — You won't fuckin' think. I'm doing all the work.

I wanted to stand up. I'd get over to the door, turn on the light. See him disappear.

I couldn't move.

— How, exactly — really — how can you say that? I asked.

— Say what?

— That you're me, I said. — What do you even mean?

— Well, I'm not going to give you a fuckin' list — a blow-by-blow account. You know, what was in the house, room by fuckin' room. The corn on the third toe on Mam's left foot. Dad's job, the uncles, aunties, any of that shite. The special gravy on Sundays. The train set, with the station Dad made for me. I'll skip all that.

— Who told you about the station —?

— I'll skip all that, he repeated. — Will I?

I nodded.

— Grand.

He stood.

— You went on the radio, he said. — When was that, Victor?

— Thirty years ago, I said. — More. Thirty-one, two — I don't know.

— And you told the chap what the Head Brother did.

— I didn't know, I said. — I thought I was the only one.

— You were.

— What?

— In that school. The only one. Before they moved him on to the next school.

— You said he did it to you too.

— Yeah. He did.

I remembered something else now.

— What about your sister? I said.

I was getting used to the darkness. I could make him out and he was the man I'd met that first time, earlier in the summer. The same clothes, the exact same clothes, and he moved now like that man too. He bent his knees and whacked his stomach.

— My sister, he said — he laughed; he growled. — For fuck sake. You remember my sister, do you?

— Yes.

— No, Victor, you don't. There's no sister. Sorry. But I knew you'd fall for it.

He bent down towards me. I could smell his breath. He was real. He stood up straight, away from me. I could have run, I could have dashed.

— I knew, he said. — I knew if I made up a girl with tits, you'd remember her and it would get me remembered as well. Because she was my sister. You remembered Eddie Fitzpatrick's sister, so you had to remember Eddie. It's so fuckin' easy. I just hinted that she mightn't have obejected to having your hands on those tits once upon a time, and you remembered her. Cos you wanted to.

He clapped his hands again.

— Flattery, he said. — Never fails. You fuckin' eejit.

— You don't have a sister.

— I do, he said. — Just not the one you remember so fuckin' fondly.

— But I do remember her.

— No, he said. — You don't.

He was right.

— What about your name? I asked him.

228

— I'll tell you, he said. — Listen and learn. Get a group of any men our age, together. Any group of lads. And ask them do they remember a chap called Eddie Fitzpatrick from school. Tell them — jog their memories — tell them he was a bit of a mad cunt. It'll take some of them a few minutes but they'll all remember him. He laughed again.

— Especially if you tell them he had a good-looking sister with a great pair of knockers. What was her name?

— Who?

— My sister, he said. — The girl you remember. What name did I tell you? That time when I told you she'd love to hear from you. Do you remember?

— No.

— No.

— What was it?

— Haven't a clue, Victor. I can't remember either. But now that I think of it, it was you who came up with Eddie. For me, like. Do you not remember?

— No.

— Yeah, he said. — Fuckin' gas. I told you to guess who I was and you said Edward. So, grand. I was going to call myself Lar, but —

He didn't laugh this time. He went to sit again but changed his mind.

— What *is* your name then? I asked.

— Ah, for fuck sake, he said. — Come on — Jesus.

He didn't sound angry now. He wasn't going to hit me.

— Where were we? he said. — You went on the radio.

— Okay.

— And do you remember what you said?

— I'd been sexually assaulted.

— Molested.

— Is that what I said?

—Yes, he said. — You said you'd been molested.

— Okay.

— Once.

—Yes.

— Just once.

—Yeah, I said. — That's right.

— Grand, he said. — Why?

—Why what?

—Why did you lie?

— I didn't lie.

— Stop being fuckin' thick, Victor.

He sat on the table again, right in front of me.

— He put his hand on your penis, he said. — That was how you described what happened.

—Yes.

— He was teaching you how to — No. He *claimed* he was teaching you how to wrestle, so you could defend yourself. He got you down on the floor. He pinned you down. Yeah?

—Yes.

— And he groped you. Did he?

—Yes.

— Once.

—Yes, I said.

— It wasn't once.

— It was.

— No.

—Why are you doing this?

— I have to, he said. — I don't have a choice. You often think about what your life would've been like if it had been a bit different. I'm right, amn't I? A dose of the oul' what-ifs. I'm right, Victor, yeah?

— Yes — I suppose so.

— What if you hadn't gone to college. What if you hadn't done the record reviews. What if you hadn't met Rachel. What if I'd written that book. What if I'd stayed closer to home. What if I hadn't turned my back on everyone who'd ever mattered to me.

He sat up. Creaked.

— You've spent years wondering what the alternative Victor would have been like. Especially recently. Haven't you?

He leaned forward and patted my left knee.

— Haven't you?

I nodded.

— Hello, he said.

He'd left his hand on the knee.

— You're looking at him.

He sat up again.

— I am you, Victor. I told you. I'm what you became. It wasn't once.

— What?

— The Head Brother. We'll give the cunt his name. Brother McIntyre. Brother McIntyre didn't grope you once. You. Me. Will I say "us"? Would that make more sense?

— Hang on, I said.

I wasn't sure if he heard me; I wasn't sure if I'd spoken.

— You're saying he groped you too?

— I'm getting a bit sick of this, Victor.

He straightened up again.

— I'll say it once more. Only the once, now. I am you. And another thing now that I think of it. You are me.

He laughed.

— You poor fucker.

— I don't understand.

— Don't blame you, man. I am what you became. I'm all your regret.

— I still don't understand.

— No.

He creaked again.

— He didn't molest you — me. Us. Once. He didn't stop there. Once. Twice. It was seventeen times. He raped us, Victor.

— No, he didn't.

— He did. And you know it. He raped you. He got your trousers down. He told you to help him. That was the killer. Because I did. I unbuckled my belt. I helped him. And he raped me. For a month. And no one said a thing. Remember?

— Yes.

— Yeah. The blood on my underpants. I tried to wash it off but there was still a stain and I couldn't throw them out cos I only had two pairs. And I even hoped Mam would notice the stain and I was scared shitless she would. The fuckin' shame — the consequences. And no one asked why I was late home from school all those times. None of the lads asked why I had to stay behind. And Dad being sick. He was a clever fucker, Brother McIntyre. Wasn't he?

I nodded. I didn't want to hear my voice. I was already listening to it.

— It wasn't my fault, he said. — Do you remember saying that? It wasn't my fault. I bet you thought that. I bet you said it. To Rachel.

I nodded again.

— What's that about, by the way? he said.

— What?

— Rachel.

There was no satisfaction in his voice, no life.

— There's no Rachel, he said.

I couldn't shake my head. I couldn't nod.

— I'm right, Victor, he said. — Amn't I?

I couldn't look at him.

— Well, there is, he said. — She's on the telly and that. Did you even meet her?

I could speak now.

— Yes.

— That's right, he said. — Outside the studio.

— Yes.

— And her van. Going back into town.

— Yes.

— And?

— I couldn't — We were going to meet.

— She liked you.

— I think so.

— She did.

— Yes.

— But you didn't go — you didn't turn up.

— No.

— You were too frightened, he said. — Of what would happen or wouldn't happen. Of touching her, yeah?

I could nod.

— And being touched, he said. — I know the feeling. Been there, Victor. Fuckin' done that. I've never had an erection. Can you believe that?

He sighed.

— All in the head, Victor. All in the head.

He sighed again.

— You made it up. The whole thing.

I looked at him.

— I'm sorry, Victor, he said. — I really am. It would've been nice, wouldn't it? Rachel.

I could see him clearly now. It wasn't a mirror. He wasn't a twin. But I was there. Our eyes. I had teeth he'd lost but the mouths were the same, a slight dimple on the right side that Rachel had told me she liked, on the way into town in her van. He was two stone heavier and a lot of that weight seemed to rest around his neck. But the faces were the same.

— I'm not supernatural, he said. — A ghost or anything. Sorry.

— What are you?

— Like I said. You. Me.

— I still don't understand.

— You and me, both. But here we are. Here I am. It wasn't my fault. You were never sure why you said it. Or thought it. Sure you weren't?

I shook my head.

234

— I'm betting most people think it — it wasn't my fault. And try to get through it. Who've been raped, I mean. The guilt. But. It was what he said.

— What?

— I'll tell you now. It was the — the eleventh time he called me to the room. I was too frightened not to go — disobeying him. Frightened of what would happen, you know. He'd call to the house. It's stupid now, thinking that. But that's now. He knew he was safe. Cos of Dad. He knew I'd never blab. He knew I'd always turn up. I'd never go home to Mam and tell her. But then he said it. "You're old enough to stop me." D'you remember?

— Yes.

— Thanks, he said. — Thanks for saying that.

I could hear him breathing.

— "You're old enough to stop me." That was the evil part. Or the most evil — the worst. When he said that. Do you remember?

— Yes.

— Yeah, he said. — He condemned us there, didn't he?

— Yeah.

We looked at each other.

— It wasn't my fault, he said. — It wasn't our fault.

— No.

— It wasn't our fault.

I was crying. I couldn't stop crying. And I can't stop.

Other titles published by Ulverscroft:

THE INVOICE

Jonas Karlsson

It's an unremarkable life, I guess, nothing special. I'm in my thirties, I work part time in a video store in Stockholm, most of my friends are busy with their families, I live alone. I suppose you?d say I have an ordinary life . . . But I love this city, and even though my flat is small it suits me, I'm comfortable here. In the summer the sun shines in through my windows at just the right angle, and I can hear all the sounds of summer life down in the street. And there's a really good ice-cream stall just near my building, which sells my favourite flavours. So, ordinary maybe, but happy. Yes, I think it's fair to say I'm a happy man. And isn't that enough?

THE CARDINAL'S MAN

M. G. Sinclair

France, 1600s: The Thirty Years War has spread across Europe, alliances are stretched to breaking point, and enemies advance on every side. And while Louis XIII sits on the throne, the real power lies with the notorious Cardinal Richelieu. Now, with Richelieu's health failing and France in grave danger, salvation may yet be found in the most unlikely form. Sebastian Morra, born into poverty and with terrible deformities, is a dwarf on a mission. Through a mixture of brains and luck, he has travelled far from his village to become a jester at the royal court. And with a talent for making enemies, he is soon drawn into the twilight world of Cardinal Richelieu, where he discovers he might just be the only man with the talents to save France from her deadliest foes.

ALL THAT SHE CAN SEE

Carrie Hope Fletcher

Cherry has a hidden talent. She can see things other people can't, and she decided a long time ago to use this skill to help others. As far as the rest of the town is concerned, she's simply the kind-hearted young woman who runs the local bakery — but in private she uses her gift to add something special to her cakes so that after just one mouthful, the townspeople start to feel better about their lives. They don't know why they're drawn to Cherry's bakery — they just know that they're safe there, and that's how Cherry likes it. And then Chase turns up and threatens to undo all the good she has done. Because it turns out Cherry is not the only one who can see what she sees . . .

SEVEN DAYS IN SUMMER

Marcia Willett

Busy mum of twins Liv is looking forward to a week at the Beach Hut in Devon, even if she feels that something's not right between her and Matt. She's sure he's just too busy at work to join them on their summer holiday . . . Baz loves having his family to stay by the sea, but when an unexpected guest arrives, he finds himself torn between the past and the future . . . Still reeling from a break-up, all Sofia wants is a quiet summer — until she meets Baz and her plans are turned upside down. She knows she's rushing into things, but could this week at the Beach Hut be the start of something new? As tensions rise over seven days in summer, the lives of the holidaymakers begin to take an unexpected turn . . .